BUT you cannot seriously mean to keep me shut up here indefinitely for so ridiculous a reason!" Russet said. "Do you imagine I shall not be missed? I daresay the search is already on."

Mr. Cameron said gently, "I think I may safely reckon that by the time any serious search is instituted, you will have been in my hands for a month or more." He studied her thoughtfully. "Though I am a bachelor myself, I have considerable faith in the matrimonial tie as the one best fitted to control foolish and headstrong young women. I have decided it would be best for you to marry."

Russet's mouth dropped open as she stared at him aghast. Surely, oh surely, he was not going to suggest that she should marry him!

Fawcett Crest Books
by Mira Stables:

THE BYRAM SUCCESSION

HONEY-POT

MARRIAGE ALLIANCE

STRANGER WITHIN THE GATES

THE SWYNDEN NECKLACE

HONEY-POT

by

Mira Stables

FAWCETT CREST • NEW YORK

For that canine Honey-pot Jai
and her attendant Court

HONEY-POT

THIS BOOK CONTAINS THE COMPLETE TEXT OF THE ORIGINAL HARDCOVER EDITION.

Published by Fawcett Crest Books, a unit of CBS Publications, the Consumer Publishing Division of CBS Inc., by arrangement with Robert Hale Limited

ISBN: 0-449-23915-2

Selection of the Doubleday Romance Library

Printed in the United States of America

10 9 8 7 6 5 4 3 2 1

Chapter One

"Russet Ingram? Oh, no! You must be bamming me."

The soft, pretty voice rose to a sharper pitch, and drew down prompt reproof on the speaker's head.

"Letty! Lower your voice, child! How often am I to tell you that a lady never raises her voice in public? Your language, too. 'Bamming', indeed! I'm sure I cannot imagine where you pick up such words. It is not as though you had brothers to lead you into habits of careless speech."

Her daughter's charming countenance was turned to hers, innocence and penitence writ plain for all the world to see. The golden head drooped a little as Letty said, "I am sorry, Mama. Is it so *very* bad? I thought it was only another word for hoaxing. I had it from Mary, I think. I daresay she picked it up from John or

Robert. I will try to remember not to use it again."

Since the Mary in question was the daughter of a Viscount and her elder brother a very eligible parti, this answer wholly appeased Mrs. Waydene's displeasure. Her slightly petulant expression turned to an indulgent smile.

"Such a sweet girl, dear Mary," she told her hostess. "She and my Lettice are the greatest of friends. Indeed, if Letty's affections had not already been engaged, I cannot help feeling that a match between her and Robert Dysart would have been quite delightful. But there is Lucinda to come out next year," she added contentedly, "and it may be"—she broke off at that point. Such solemn matters were not for young ears. She turned back to the two girls who had been exchanging confidences in the window seat. "And what has Barbara been saying, that you should accuse her of hoaxing you?" she wanted to know.

"Why! She tells me that it is Russet Ingram who is the toast of the town—the famous 'honey-pot' who has taken society by storm. And indeed I found it hard to believe, Mama. I daresay *you* will find it difficult even to recall her appearance. She was the junior governess at Mrs. Selmerdine's though she did not come much in my way. You may remember her sister, Joanna, who is a little younger than I and very pretty. Miss Ingram, too, had been a pupil at the Academy. The other girls said that Mrs. Selmerdine kept her on as a governess out of kindness when her Papa lost his money."

She did not add that the kindness—or so her fellow pupils had agreed—was for Miss Ingram's Papa. One did not say such things to Mama. She would find it pert and disagreeable. It would blemish her mental image of a sweetly ingenuous little daughter, an image that Letty had been at some pains to nourish and preserve.

Mama was nodding her head reflectively. "I certainly remember the Ingram débacle," she said slowly. "A fortune gamed away in a night, or so the story ran. Though I daresay there had been some pretty deep doings before that." It occurred to her that here was another subject unsuited to the tender ears of innocence. She turned to her hostess with a request that the girls should be permitted to stroll through the conservatories for a while.

Mrs Mansfield was very willing. There was a good deal of pleasure to be got from bringing out a daughter, especially one so successful as her Barbara, who had obliged her by contracting a very eligible alliance during this, her first season. But there could be no denying that the young were very much in the way when one wanted to enjoy a comfortable gossip. She waited only until the girls had gone before enquiring in deeply interested tones, "And when may we expect to see the announcement of Lettice's betrothal?"

Mrs Waydene preened a little. "It is not quite settled," she explained. "Lucian's parents wish to give a dress ball to celebrate the event, and it would be improper for them to do so before they have put off their blacks for his grandpapa. I should think perhaps next month. Otherwise people will be leaving Town for the summer. But I tell Lucian there is no great hurry for the marriage. I am not so anxious to part with my treasure. She has been the greatest comfort to me since her Papa died and I really don't know how I shall go on without her. Which makes it so very fortunate that she should have set her heart on Lucian. It will be delightful having her so close at hand. Indeed it was *that* circumstance which reconciled me to the match, for it cannot be said to be a brilliant one, you know. To be sure, his fortune is handsome. But the estate is not large, and the house is pretty rather than distinguished. A mere baronet, too. Since we are quite alone, I need not scruple to say that I think my pretty Letty might have looked higher. But she had been attached to him ever since she was a mere schoolgirl, and he, of course, dotes on her. I had not the heart to refuse my consent."

That at least one could believe, thought Mrs Mansfield shrewdly; with two more daughters on her hands and the younger one as freckled as a plover's egg, though Lucinda, at least, was more that passably pretty. She herself was *not* a besotted parent and acknowledged that though her Barbara was sensible and pleasant mannered she was no more than well to pass in point of beauty, while Letty Waydene was the answer to a mother's prayers, deliciously feminine with her golden curls and big blue eyes, her modest bearing and demure ways. There was a touch of malice in her voice as she said, on a tiny sigh, "Our girls must think themselves fortunate to have received even *respectable* offers while there is a Russet Ingram to turn the heads of all the most eligible bachelors in Town."

Fortunately for the smoothness of their further relationship, Mrs Waydene was sufficiently interested in Miss Ingram to overlook the slight to her darling. She said slowly, as one dredging up memories of some insignificant happening, "I think I *do* remember the girl. Thin and colourless, save for her hair, and, I should have said, totally lacking in feminine appeal. For once I am inclined to agree with Letty. Are you sure that you are not hoaxing me?"

Mrs Mansfield smiled. "Quite sure. Wait till you see her. I think you have not allowed for the gilding that wealth and good taste can bestow upon even a thin and colourless female. I doubt if another woman would ever describe

Miss Ingram as good looking, but no one, now, would call her colourless. That copper coloured hair of hers was probably a disaster in a penniless governess. To a girl who is always beautifully dressed in colours and materials that set it off to perfection, it becomes a distinguishing feature which stamps her as something out of the common. And her charm is undeniable. Even her rivals admit it. While as for her manners, she conducts herself with an unassuming simplicity that cannot fail to please."

"A paragon indeed," said Mrs Waydene with something of a snap. "And a handsome fortune, of course!"

"So I believe. It is generally understood that the uncle left his money equally between the two sisters, which would make them both substantial heiresses."

"Then it seems strange that this one has not married. If memory serves me she must be three or four and twenty. At this rate, for all her fortune and this much vaunted charm, she will end up an ape leader."

Mrs Mansfield shrugged. "If she does, it will not be from lack of opportunity to change her state. Though naturally she herself does not speak of it, she must have refused some splendid offers. The gentlemen themselves make no secret of it. Indeed Mr Mansfield tells me that they lay bets in the clubs as to which of them will win the prize."

"Disgusting," snorted her listener.

"Indeed! But scarcely Miss Ingram's fault," pointed out Mrs Mansfield. "Any mother with daughters to dispose of cannot but wish that she would make her choice, for it is quite true that the men are round her like bees round a honey-pot—which is how she came by that ridiculous nickname—but I must admit that she is a delightful girl. She showed Barbara great kindness when she made her come-out. You know how gauche and stiff a débutante can be. Miss Ingram invited her to one or two small informal parties which were not so alarming as the grander functions, took her driving in the park several times and introduced her to a number of unexceptionable young gentlemen, so that she soon began to feel herself more at home in the social scene. Both Barbara and I have good cause to be grateful to her."

This honest tribute only stirred Mrs Waydene to deeper disapproval. "To me there is something very objectionable about so young a female assuming the rights and privileges of an established hostess," she announced firmly. "To be giving her own parties, inviting just such friends as she chooses, patronising younger girls, seems to me presumptuous to the point of arrogance. But of course she is of dubious ancestry, is she not? The Ingrams are above criticism I am well aware, but did not Ralph Ingram marry some foreigner? French or Spanish, I think. And who is to say what kind of family *she* came from?"

"He married the only daughter of a noble Siennese family," returned Mrs Mansfield drily, "and was thought to have done very well for himself. If Miss Ingram has cause to be ashamed of either of her parents, it is certainly not her Mama. Ralph Ingram is a charming good-for-naught who squandered a respectable inheritance in gambling and other disreputable pursuits too improper to mention. It is an open secret that his uncle's fortune came to the two girls on condition that he reside permanently in Italy where adequate provision was made for his comfort. And it is at least to his credit that he did not object to such a humiliating arrangement. I believe he is a very likeable creature. His wife adored him to her dying day, despite his flagrant infidelities, and the two girls visit him regularly."

Mrs Waydene looked more sour than ever. "You are very loyal," she said in disparaging tones. "I suppose Miss Ingram has a chaperone? Or is she, perhaps, beyond the age of needing one?"

Her hostess laughed. "Not quite," she said temperately, remembering that she *was* the hostess; though why she had troubled to keep up her acquaintance with her old school fellow she really could not imagine. "A widowed cousin lives with them—there is a younger sister, you know, only just out." And dared not add that Joanna Ingram was thought to have brought off the catch of the season. It was not yet announced, but the girl was to spend a month at a certain ducal residence, which surely indicated which way the wind lay. She managed to turn the talk to the vast expense of bringing out a daughter, a topic which appealed very much to Mrs Waydene since, she confided, the cost of Letty's belated début was to be met by her guardian and trustee, who had also promised to lend his Town house for the grand ball which was to inaugurate several weeks of gaiety.

Now if one was to talk of breeding and of inherited characteristics, thought Mrs Mansfield while her guest ran on about Mr Cameron's generosity, *that* gentleman must have some interesting possibilities. On the father's side he was descended from a scion of Clan Cameron, one of those unfortunate gentlemen who had supported the Stuart cause in the 'Fifteen rising and had followed his king into exile. A Highland gentleman, proud as the devil no doubt, brooking no opposition to his will. And as though that were not enough, he—or perhaps it was his son, she could not precisely remember—had married a Polish lady. A Countess, some said, though she, too, was an exile since one or other of the interminable wars that had ravaged her unhappy country. The present James Cameron was something of a mystery. Apart from his friendship with the late Mr Waydene, a friendship stemming from a chance encounter in India, little was known of him. He seemed to be a man of wealth, since he had a house in Leicestershire and another in Hampshire as well as the Town house. He kept magnificent horses, too, but apart from this showed no particular signs of affluence. He was no gamester and took little part in the round of functions which filled every waking hour during the season. She enquired politely if he would be playing host for Letty's ball, but Mrs Waydene seemed to think it unlikely. He had given her carte blanche to make all the arrangements but had been evasive about his own movements on the all-important night, saying that he might not be returned from Hampshire and that she had better secure the support of her brother, Letty's other guardian, to oversee the comfort of the male guests.

"Not that one really needs a host for that kind of party," explained Mrs Waydene judicially. "It is not as if there was to be any gaming. A card party is all very well in its way, but I do not intend to have half the gentlemen vanishing into the card room at my daughter's ball."

Mrs Mansfield, who would not have

dreamed of giving a party which did not offer some form of entertainment for such of her guests as did not care for dancing, nodded sagely, and thought it would take a very determined gentleman indeed to withstand Emily's hectoring ways. She did not wonder at James Cameron's evasive tactics, but could not help hoping that he would change his mind about appearing at his ward's ball. Since she had never previously chanced to meet him, his presence would relieve the tedium of a long evening spent in exchanging all the usual platitudes with the usual band of dutiful chaperones.

Mrs Waydene began to gather up gloves and reticule preparatory to departure. An abigail was despatched to find the young ladies and tell Miss Waydene that her Mama was ready to leave.

The conversation in the conservatories had also touched briefly on Miss Ingram. Letty's ecstatic description of the gown that she was to wear for the ball had led to a long and exhaustive discussion of the wardrobes of both young ladies, and Barbara's remarks had been punctuated from time to time by such phrases as, "and Miss Ingram says I should never wear pink, except the very palest shades," or, wistfully, "I would dearly love just such a gown as that, but Miss Ingram advised against satin because it would make me look plump."

It was natural, then, that when at last the absorbing topic of dress had palled a little, Letty should say, "You seem to set a good deal of store by Russet Ingram's opinion. Do tell me more about her. I cannot picture her as a society belle."

Barbara was nothing loath. She had conceived a great admiration for the older girl which had developed into sincere affection. She was happy to talk of her, extolling her kindness and describing various toilets that she had worn, praising her wit and her accomplishments and, inevitably, referring to the way that she held court, with attentive gentlemen hurrying to forestall her lightest wish. She did not notice that Letty, her curiosity soon appeased, had begun to look first bored and then distinctly petulant. Presently she broke in rather rudely upon her friend's account of a theatre party and the number of gentlemen who had crowded not only Miss Ingram's box but also the corridor that led to it, saying with a tiny artificial yawn, "Indeed a diamond of the first water—as Mama would *not* permit me to say. And all the gentlemen so besotted! It must be as amusing as a play. But I can tell you of one man, at least, who will not succumb to her spell, charm she never so wisely," and her mouth curved to a little smile of triumph.

Barbara stared at her, her soft pink lips half

open in protest at this gross misrepresentation of her friend's character. Miss Ingram did *not* deliberately strive to enmesh her many admirers. It was just that she was so appealing, so sympathetic and so comically entertaining, too. But Letty did not wait to hear. She went on confidently, "All the rest of the world may bow down and worship her if they will. But not my Lucian. If I am by his side, he will not even be aware of her existence. No, not even if she were to single him out for her particular favour. He has eyes only for me."

Chapter Two

"An excellent choice, love. You look quite delightfully. The brocade has made up even better than I thought and the hoop is *quite* large enough. Any wider and it would have appeared clumsy. But not that fan, do you think?"

Miss Joanna Ingram looked down regretfully at the fan which hung from one slender wrist. Its creamy silk fabric was a perfect match for the deeper hue that showed in the folds of the brocade, and its delicate design of birds and flowers in soft tones of pink and blue and mauve was exactly to her youthful taste.

"You gave it to me yourself," she pointed out hopefully, "and I have always liked it the best of all my fans."

Russet smiled. "So I did, my dear. And that is just why. It would be more tactful to carry the parchment one that the Duchess gave you, which also goes well with your dress even if it is not quite so pretty. *She* would be gratified to see you using it, and Gilbert will be pleased by anything that pleases his Mama. He is truly devoted to her, you know, and I am sure it is an object with you to win his approval, even in so small a matter."

Joanna's face lit to the mere suggestion. She was deliciously transparent, thought Russet, half pityingly. Heaven send that nothing occurred to blight her innocent happiness. She was so young, so defenceless, all her heart given to her adored Gilbert. And so far as the man himself was concerned, Russet knew no fears. She had learned a good deal about gentlemen during the two years of her reign over London's social whirl, even if she had not yet met the one for whom she would willingly surrender her spinster freedom. Joanna had chosen wisely. It was the attitude of Gilbert's parents that gave her sister some cause for concern. They had been kind. But the kindness had been cool, reserved. And Russet suspected that this temperate welcome was of deliberate policy. Outright opposition would probably have estranged their son, made him all the more determined to marry Joanna, for he was no weakling. The Duchess was probably relying upon the close attachment between herself and Gilbert to help her dissuade him from a match which she could not wholly approve. In all fairness, Russet could not honestly blame her. Joanna herself was unexceptionable—

well-born, well-dowered and so deep in love as to be willing to learn eagerly all the difficult lessons that would be part of her training for the great state that she would some day enjoy. If enjoyment was an accurate description, thought her sister wryly. But what great family would wish for so close an association with the black sheep of the Ingrams? What parents, with a succession to consider, could fail to wonder whether Papa's wildness might not come out in the innocent Joanna or her off-spring? The invitation to spend a month at Denholme had been a significant advance. Gilbert must indeed be pressing his parents hard. But it had not included Joanna's sister. The Duchess was doubtless anxious to see how the girl conducted herself when the restraining influence of elder sister and Cousin Olivia was removed.

Russet had no anxieties on that score. There was not a scrap of artifice in Joanna's makeup. She was sound and sweet as a bell and would ring true however she was tested, while the diffidence natural to youth and inexperience would probably make a stronger appeal to the Duchess than a poised and competent social manner.

"Powder becomes you, too," she told her sister, clever fingers coaxing one rebellious curl to conformity. "You look like a princess in the old fairy tales." And even allowing for sisterly partiality there was considerable truth in the assertion, for the snowy coiffeur lent a touch of enchantment to apple blossom skin and dark blue eyes, while first love had added its own bloom to the girl's natural radiance. "I could wish I were coming with you. But at least I need not wear powder to Letty Waydene's ball."

It was Joanna's turn to contemplate her sister's appearance. Russet had chosen to wear a dress in the bergère style, the overdress of brocade in a shade of soft yellow, a shade that was repeated in the tiny golden fleur-de-lys that were embroidered on the white satin underdress. It was vastly becoming, and Joanna felt that it was a sad pity that Gilbert's Mama would undoubtedly frown upon a style of costume which permitted the display of slim silk-clad ankles and tiny golden slippers.

"If I had hair like yours, I don't think I would ever wear powder—except to go to Court, of course," she told Russet. "And I like the way Agnes has dressed your hair tonight. It makes you look taller, piled up like that, and just the one ringlet to soften the severity. And to show how white your skin is," she added with a mischievous twinkle.

Russet grinned. "You know too much, my child," she said, mock-severe. "But I shall certainly miss Agnes when she goes with you to Denholme. I doubt if anyone else could have turned such a plain, unpromising piece into one of the smarts. If you follow her advice in the matter of dress you may rest easy on that head. Her taste is impeccable. But more than that, she seems to have an instinctive sense of occasion. Which reminds me that I had best set about engaging a new maid to take with me on my travels. It is not every girl who is willing to adventure abroad, so it may be some time before I am suited."

"I feel very guilty, depriving you of Agnes," Joanna said, "but she will be the greatest comfort to me so I shall not press you to change your mind."

"Nor I pay any heed to such a foolish suggestion," returned Russet lightly. "It will be the greatest comfort to *me*, too, to know that you have her with you at Denholme. But we must not be loitering here. The chairs will be waiting. I daresay I shall be very late tonight. You are not to wait up for me, remember."

Joanna dropped her a playful curtsey. "No, ma'am," she said demurely. "I wonder if your latest admirer will escort you home."

"Young Lucian?" queried Russet, smiling. "He's a pleasant lad—full of chivalry and lofty ideals. I like him. I wonder if it is true that he is as good as promised to Letty Waydene. Perhaps there will be an announcement tonight, though I always feel that it is rather a pity to announce one's betrothal at a coming out ball.

Anyway, he's no admirer of mine. Just because he chanced to come to the rescue when that horrid dog set upon poor Doll. Cousin Olivia would never have forgiven me if any harm had befallen her precious pug. What could I do but invite him to come in so that she might thank him herself? And then to find out that she was acquainted with his Mama. To be sure he had no need to send us flowers, but that is just the kind of charming attention to which he has been bred, and means nothing. I'll thank you not to make mischief by exaggerating the importance of a boy's innocent gallantries."

Joanna wrinkled a pretty little nose at her, quite unrepentant. "I know," she confessed. "But I cannot help feeling that it would do Letty Waydene a great deal of good to see her beau paying attention to some other female. She is a spiteful little cat, for all her sugary ways. If Lucian Staneborough is as nice as you say, he is by far too good for her. I daresay he thinks she is as sweet as she looks. But I was at school with her and I know better."

Russet looked rueful. "I'll admit I've no great liking for her myself. Or rather that I did not care for her above half when she was a well-to-do pupil and I a penniless governess. She was one of the few girls who made me feel my inferior status. But perhaps she has improved. If she has fallen in love with that charming boy it must surely have sweetened her disposition! And remember that I *did* receive an invitation to her ball."

Joanna bestowed an indulgent smile upon her as she drew the white velvet cape about her shoulders. "Because Mrs Waydene knows very well that no function is complete unless Miss Ingram is among the guests," she said calmly, and would have gone on to speculate about the reactions of various notable gentlemen of the 'ton' if they had been required to suffer such deprivation, had not Agnes tapped on the door to say that the chairs had been awaiting their passengers for close on half an hour.

Borne along steadily in her chair, Russet contemplated the evening ahead of her with only tepid pleasure. She was growing spoiled, she decided, for two short years ago she would have found the prospect enthralling. But really one ball was very like another, and the same could be said of so many of the functions on which hostesses spent so much time and trouble. One met the same people, exchanged the same banalities. She still derived considerable pleasure from dressing herself becomingly. She thought she probably always would. The years of penny pinching had seen to that, and the very fact that she was by no means beautiful presented a constant challenge. To have made herself a leader of fashion when she was so far removed from the popular ideal of feminine beauty was no small achievement. Her eyes were good—golden hazel, darkly fringed and set under slender arching brows; and her skin, as Joanna had teased her, was creamy smooth, even if it lacked the rose petal transparency so much admired and so desperately counterfeited. But she was too small and too slight for an age that admired opulence. 'A rare plump armful,' was the masculine ideal. A woman should be cuddlesome and yielding, and Russet was neither. The wide mouth and the wilful chin with its determined cleft were silent witnesses to her true nature. Generous, loving and loyal she might be, but she had a mind of her own and scant patience with pretension or pomposity. Masculine complacency was like to receive short shrift at her hands.

Her thoughts turned for a moment to Lucian Staneborough. Nothing of that sort about him. A thoroughly nice youngster. Had she been his sister she would be very proud of him she thought, and smiled to herself in the darkness at the realisation that her feelings towards him bordered on the maternal. How Joanna would laugh! To be sure she probably *was* a couple of years the older, but far more unequal matches were made every day. In her case, of course, a match was not even in question. She wondered once again if ever she would meet a man to whom she could give her heart. It seemed unlikely. For two years now she had queened it over London's eligibles; had received more offers than a modest girl cared to remember. Not once had her deeper emotions been touched though she had liked some of her suitors pretty well. Not well enough to wish to spend the rest of her life with them, though. So what was she to do with herself? If the delights of the season had lost their charm, how should she fill her days?

She hoped that she was as charitable as the next but she had no great urge to devote herself to good works. Foreign travel, then? That held more appeal. She had always enjoyed her visits to Papa. But to enjoy new sights and scenes to the full one really needed a sympathetic companion, and that was not so easily arranged. In fact there were a good many difficulties in the path of the would-be traveller if she was young, single and female.

The bearers stopped and set the chair down. Russet abandoned speculation about the future and stepped out on to the carpet that had been laid over the flag-way for the convenience of Mrs Waydene's guests.

Mrs Waydene could have no cause for complaint about the setting for her daughter's début. Mr Cameron's house in fashionable Cavendish Square was magnificently furnished, and if the critical Miss Ingram thought it a little on the sombre side it certainly served to set off the elegant costumes of the guests who crowded the reception rooms and stood gossiping in groups on the elegant staircase. Perhaps the ballroom was a little small for such a grand affair, but there were galleries at both ends where one could watch the dancing if one so chose, and though no other form of entertainment was offered so lavish were the refreshments, so varied the choice of wines, that even the habitual card players forebore to complain. After all, there was some amusement to be found in discussing their absent host and in estimating the extent of his fortune. Judging by the state he kept, by the displays of porcelain and ivories and other curios and objets d'art too numerous to mention, it must be immense. There were servants always at hand to offer refreshments and replenish glasses. Barbara Mansfield, chattering gaily with Russet during an interval between the dances, was filled with admiration.

"I'm disappointed in one thing, though," she confided. "I expected Indian servants. Letty says her guardian spent many years in the East where he has business interests, and that when he came home for good he brought most of his household with him."

Waiting her turn to go down the set in the country dance, Russet wondered if it was the Eastern influence that she found rather strange. One could not say the rooms were over-furnished, for everything was in perfect harmony, nor yet that the hangings and the colours were too exotic, though the use of gold and peacock blue was certainly striking. With so much panelling and the dark carved furniture—ebony she supposed it was—the vivid colour was soon muted. It was not like her to be fanciful, but she sensed an atmosphere in the magnificent rooms that seemed to pose some enigmatic threat. It made her wary, distrait, so that she almost forgot the sequence of the figures until the surprised face of her partner recalled her to a proper regard for her social responsibilities and she apologised so prettily that the poor young man took fresh heart. Never had his lady seemed so approachable. He began to ponder the possibility of persuading her to stroll with him in the conservatory.

Miss Lettice Waydene watched Russet's progress jealously. No one could fault the guest's decorum. She would not even dance twice with the same partner, and *that* was perfectly permissible. Yet gentlemen's heads turned whenever she went by, her name was on everyone's lips, and if the murmurs of admiration were occasionally spiced with jealousy, they were none the less sincere. Letty could see nothing in her, except a certain dignity and grace of deportment—and that, she thought, was only because of those endless boring lessons which had been her one link with Miss Ingram in her schooldays. Yet Lucian—*her Lu-*

cian—had actually expressed his admiration for the creature. Letty had always disliked her; had treated her with contempt when it had seemed safe to do so. Now she felt that she actually hated her; would like nothing better than to see her humiliated and brought low. How dare she draw all eyes in the room to herself—her mediocre self—thought Letty indignantly, very conscious of her own far superior claims to attention!

She had not so very long to wait. Lucian, not realising the magnitude of the privilege, had requested Miss Ingram's hand for the first cotillion. And since the request had been made some time before the day of the ball, no one had forestalled him. Letty chanced to be standing close by Russet as he came to claim his dance. It was then that her jealousy prompted her to put out her hand to him and say sweetly, "Ah! You are here. Do you know, I almost thought you had forgotten me. Shall we join Barbara's set?"

She was—and well she knew it—engaged to dance this first set with her uncle. But he was very easy-going and would not fuss or scold her for what was, after all, a very natural mistake. It was the *second* cotillion, with supper to follow, that was promised to Lucian. Uncle Percival was not even in sight, so why should she not take the wind out of Miss Ingram's eye?

Lucian's face was a study in embarrassment.

He was not very old and his social poise was scarcely equal to the occasion. He stammered something slightly incoherent about a mistake and glanced appealingly at Russet.

Letty's big blue eyes were lifted to his in limpid innocence. "Oh no! I could not mistake *our* dance," she told him soulfully. And then, on a note that was almost a wail, "You cannot mean to let me be a wallflower at my very own ball! If there is a mistake I am sure Miss Ingram will hold you excused."

Russet's predominant emotion was pity for the poor young man. She masked her indignation at what was nothing more than bare-faced piracy and turned to him a face of amused acquiescence. "By all means," she said coolly. "I shall be perfectly happy to stroll in the galleries for a while and have the opportunity of studying some of the curious and beautiful objects with which they are adorned."

Lucian's face relaxed into undisguised relief. He felt that Letty's behaviour was unbecoming, even if she really *had* made a mistake, but she was very young, he reflected tenderly, and no doubt the evening's excitement had gone to her head. He loved her dearly. But even as he offered his arm to lead her into the set that was just forming he was meditating the gentle rebuke that he must presently administer. Thanks to Miss Ingram's compliance on this occasion, an ugly scene had been avoided, but he would still have to make his apologies for appearing to slight one who had shown him nothing but kindness. Letty must be taught that her behaviour was unworthy of a lady with any claim to gentility.

Unfortunately Letty was not content to rest on so easy a triumph. She must needs venture another pin-prick. Taking Russet's easy disclaimer at face value she said patronisingly, "I daresay you will be very glad of the chance to sit down and rest. Mama is for ever wondering where I find the energy to dance a whole evening away. As one grows older I believe it is a positive relief not to be obliged to dance every number."

Russet laughed outright. Such an exhibition of spite was *too* ridiculous. To be classed with the dowagers at her age—and she positively besieged by admirers at every function she attended—was more comical than hurtful. Not even poor Lucian's horrified face could check her merriment. Indeed she hoped he would deal faithfully with the horrid little wretch, though more for his own sake than for any fancied wrongs of hers. If his intentions in that direction were as serious as rumour hinted, then it would do no harm to take Miss Waydene in hand before her disposition was utterly ruined by her doting Mama. For the moment the best she could do for him was to turn away, still smiling, and leave him to conduct the triumphant Letty to her place in the set.

Naturally the matter could not be allowed to rest there. Over supper Lucian spoke so sternly to his partner on the evils that stemmed from lack of conduct that even Miss Letty's conceit of herself was sadly dashed. She could scarcely believe it that Lucian should take such a tone with her, but to speak truth she found it vastly exciting to see him so determined and unyielding. He looked so handsome that it quite made her heart flutter. One could not cry in public, of course, even if one was among the select band who could do so prettily, but the big blue eyes were huge and misty, the soft mouth dropped pathetically. But since this penitent attitude accorded ill with an absolute refusal to beg Miss Ingram's pardon, it wholly failed of its intent. She might *look* wistful and submissive, but she stuck to it that she had spoken nothing but the truth and could see no cause to humble herself. The rift between the pair widened appreciably. Lucian said that if she would not apologise herself he must do so on her behalf. This was very ill received. Letty, whose soft exterior covered a mulish obstinacy, tossed her head and vowed he might do as he pleased.

It never occurred to her that such behaviour might tarnish her image in his eyes. On the contrary, she was quite enjoying their first tiff.

He had always been so adoring—almost reverent—treating her as though she was something fragile and precious. She had never seen him in this sterner, more masculine guise. She decided that she would show him that he could not take her so much for granted. He should suffer a little before she graciously took him back into favour. She went off to conduct a discreet flirtation with Robert Dysart, concerned only that Lucian should have every opportunity of observing her manoeuvres.

Lucian's mood was vastly different. It was his first glimpse of the unpleasant side of his beloved and it shook him sadly. He was not even aware of Mistress Letty's skilled skirmishing, his mind more concerned with her apparent inability to realise the shocking nature of her conduct. His partners found him polite but not forthcoming. He was unable to make an opportunity for private speech with Miss Ingram but felt that he must do so as soon as possible, and with this object in view he waited in the hall for her departure. She was one of the last to leave, detained several times as she came down the magnificent staircase by friends who wished to confirm some projected plan or suggest some pleasurable engagement, so it was late indeed before Lucian found the opportunity he sought.

"Miss Ingram—I beg of you—not here and now, of course, it is not the time or place—but I must have speech with you. Pray grant me leave. May I call on you tomorrow?"

Russet surveyed him with compassion. Just the kind of high-bred chivalrous boy to be foolishly distressed by that trivial incident in the ballroom.

"Yes, of course," she said soothingly. "But it might be better if we rode together in the park —or I will drive out with you if you prefer that. So we may talk at our ease, for I think that the subject you are so anxious to discuss is not intended for Cousin Olivia's ears."

She smiled at him sympathetically. He was moved to take her hand and raise it to his lips. "I might have known you would understand," he told her gratefully. "I will call for you, then, tomorrow morning, and you shall give me your opinion of my new pair." With which gallant attempt at lightness he kissed her hand again and strode out into the comforting darkness, while Russet sank back thankfully into the waiting chair. Neither of them noticed the tall dark gentleman who had just deposited hat and whip on an ancient chest that stood in one corner of the hall, though *he* eyed the pair with mild curiosity, being unable to avoid hearing what passed between them. Rather a forward piece, thought Mr Cameron idly, appointing a gentleman to meet her where they could not be overheard by a chaperone with no more ado that *he* would have made over an appointment with his agent. But it was no concern of his. He dismissed the pair from his mind and strolled into his library which had been kept blessedly free from the evening's festivities, there to look through such correspondence as had accumulated during his absence.

Chapter Three

Instinct warned Letty that it would be worse than useless to employ artifice in her approach to her guardian. For once in her scheming little life she had been taken completely at fault. Lucian had not responded in at all the way that she had expected. There were no furious outbursts of jealousy, no demonstrations of possessive passion. He did not neglect her; he was scrupulously polite. He simply ignored the rivals whom she chose to parade for his subjugation and his manner was gently withdrawn. He refused to discuss Miss Ingram beyond saying that he had apologised to the lady for her unintentional discourtesy—a remark that made her writhe in impotent fury—but she was very well aware that the two of them were on the friendliest of terms. Barbara Mansfield had actually seen them driving in the park on the very morning after her ball, and she herself had seen them dancing together on more than one occasion. No one could say that Lucian had singled out Miss Ingram for more attention than any other girl, and it was so much the fashion for gentlemen to dangle after her that no one paid any particular attention to this latest addition to her court, but Letty was bitterly jealous of every glance that he bestowed upon her rival—for so she chose to phrase it. What was worse, he had made no more mention of announcing their betrothal in the Gazette, and even Mama was beginning to be restive over this, asking if she had done anything to displease him. As if she would! And she so deep in love, the more so because Lucian was being a little difficult. It was all Russet Ingram's fault, decided Letty angrily. She had deliberately set herself out to beguile Lucian away from his allegiance, and that out of sheer malice. Not even Letty believed that she had serious matrimonial designs on him. Grudgingly she admitted that Miss Ingram could do far better for herself. So she could only be activated by jealousy and spite because Letty was so much the prettier.

This, at any rate, was the version of the tale that she poured out to Mr Cameron. The beginning of the story she deliberately left rather sketchy. Her guardian, she felt, would not wish to be troubled with the details of the original dispute. He listened patiently enough. By now he had met Lucian Staneborough on several occasions. He would have been inclined to like the boy, save for that unfortunate first encounter on the night of Letty's ball. As a man of principle it did not seem to him at all the thing for a young gentleman as good as betrothed to one girl to be making urgent assignations with another. Not being a patron of social squeezes he had not had the privilege of meeting Miss Ingram, but he had heard a good deal about her and had no hesitation in identifying her as the young lady of the urgent assignation. A forward piece he had thought her and it seemed that he had been right. Now, if he was to believe Letty's rambling tale, she was also a mischief-maker, actuated by nothing stronger than idle malice.

When the tale was done he said sensibly, "Well, my dear, I am truly sorry for your unhappiness, but just what were you hoping that I could do about it? To be sure I promised my aid when you said you were in a difficulty, but short of pressing Staneborough to declare his intentions—and that, I gather, is *not* your desire—it does not seem to me to be a man's business. Can not your Mama advise you?"

Letty lifted a woe-begone face to his. Her distress was not feigned. She had begun to fear that her conduct had seriously estranged Lucian. "I dare not tell Mama," she confessed. "She would be so angry with me. She would be bound to say that I had made a mull of the whole business, just when it was in a fair way to being settled. You see she wants to bring Lucinda out next year, and then there is Cecily to be thought of. She is anxious that I should be properly established before then."

That was plain speaking with a vengeance, thought her guardian wryly. He was not sure that he cared for such a materialistic approach. The child seemed more concerned with her social prospects than with her broken heart. Not that he would have cared for a display of hysterical sentimentality. He knit his brows over the problem.

"Perhaps a charming new gown?" he suggested. "I am not well versed in such matters but I imagine that it might have a beneficial effect. And if you have out-run the constable," he ended kindly, "it would be my pleasure to make you a gift of just such a gown. I would suggest something soft and clinging in white, with blue ribands. Surely the sight of you so attired would soften the hardest heart."

But Letty shook her head dolefully, and it was the measure of her distress that she did not even make the most of such a golden opportunity. "You are very kind," she said sadly. "But I tried it—only the gown was palest pink—and it did not serve in the least."

She looked as though she might burst into tears. Her guardian surveyed her curiously. He had not previously paid her much attention.

Mrs Waydene he frankly disliked, avoiding her as much as was consistent with his interpretation of his duty, and Letty had seemed to him just a pretty child with rather less sense than a kitten. It now appeared that she had more depth than he had credited to her.

He said soberly, "Do you love him so very much?" and wondered even as he said it what this piece of pink and white daintiness could understand of love.

Letty looked surprised. Of course she loved Lucian. He was suitable in every particular—well-born, wealthy and handsome. And until that horrid Russet Ingram had crossed his path he had treated his Letty with the reverence due to a goddess. Now it was all spoiled. She ignored the fact that it was her own folly rather than Russet's behaviour that had begun the trouble and that she cared a good deal more for Lucian now that she seemed to stand in danger of losing him. Her lip trembled piteously, but she made a valiant effort to hold back the tears since Mama had impressed upon her that there was nothing that gentlemen disliked so much as a weeping female.

"Yes," she said baldly, in a voice that was husky from her effort to control it. "I do."

In fact Mama's advice served her well. Not that Mr Cameron would have been embarrassed by her tears. He would simply have mopped her up and comforted her as he might a child. But her difficulty in uttering the simplest words without breaking down prevented her from launching into the passionate appeal that she had planned, in which she would mention the probability of her early demise if she could not marry Lucian, either from a decline or a broken heart—she had not quite decided which—and, had she but known it, her simple avowal was far more convincing.

Her guardian thrust a hand distractedly through his carefully arranged dark locks—he shared with Miss Ingram at least one foible of which both were unaware, in that never, save to attend Court, would he wear either powder or a wig. "I still don't see how I can be of any assistance," he said slowly.

There was desperation in Letty's glance. She said it timidly, but she said it. "I wondered if perhaps you could pay court to her—Miss Ingram. Draw her off, you know." And then, not realising how she was betraying herself, "You are very wealthy, are you not? I know that Miss Ingram was much impressed by the house and your collections. And you are really very good-looking, for an older man," she added kindly, with an air of patronage that was irresistibly funny. "Moreover," she went on, warming to her task, "it is said of you that you are not interested in females, and that, you know, presents a challenge that such a woman as Miss Ingram might well find intriguing. Do you not think that, for Papa's sake"—that came out of her rehearsed speech—"you could strive to engage her interest just until I"—at which point she faltered into silence. Not even to a sympathetic audience could she bring herself to add, "until I have Lucian safe." And she doubted if her guardian was as sympathetic as he had at first appeared, for he had thrown back that handsome dark head of his—and he *was*, indeed, very good-looking—and was laughing consumedly.

Letty, who could see nothing humorous in her artless summary of his attractions, stared at him offendedly. He controlled his mirth, assured her politely that he was well known for his odd sense of the ridiculous, and said that, although he was not sufficiently conceited to believe himself capable of diverting Miss Ingram's attention from Staneborough, yet it was an approach that suggested certain possibilities. He would think the matter over and would see if something could not be contrived that might serve equally well. With that she had to be content. But since he then repeated his offer of a new gown, she allowed herself to be fobbed off without further enquiry.

When she was gone Mr Cameron applied himself seriously to the problem. His sense of responsibility was strong and unfortunately it insisted that, had Letty's Papa been alive, he would certainly have made some attempt at mediation. As matters stood it was his plain duty to intervene. And a tricksy awkward business it was. He was perfectly willing to do all that he could for his three wards in the way of seeing that they were properly cared for and provided with every comfort, but this feminine manoeuvring was not at all to his taste. A delicate approach to Miss Ingram was obviously indicated, and Mr Cameron, who had never had the time for much commerce with the opposite sex, was doubtful of his abilities in this direction. However it must be attempted. He began to con the ranks of his friends in search of someone who might be acquainted with the lady and willing to present him—and realised anew the awkwardness of the situation. Even if he could find someone to oblige him in this way, he wanted no third party present at the interview that would follow. He began to think more kindly of Miss Ingram's notion of driving in the park if one wanted to confer with a gentleman privately on a matter of some delicacy. In fact he could not think of any better scheme. And since there was no great urgency about the business—save for his own desire to be done with it as soon as possible—he took to driving in the park every afternoon, taking up such of his friends as he knew to be acquainted with Miss Ingram in the hope of a fortuitous meeting.

He had to wait a fortnight. By that time his

patience was more than a little threadbare. To be sure he usually exercised one or other of his magnificent teams each afternoon, but parading in the park, stopping every ten minutes or so to exchange greetings with the other idlers was not his notion of enjoyment. Unfortunately it was a bad day for Russet, too. She found herself wishing that the season was at an end, though she had still to complete her arrangements for travelling to Rome and had not yet been successful in finding a suitable maid to take Agnes's place on the journey. The trouble was her uneasy state of mind over Joanna's future. She was well aware that any breath of scandal that touched her sister now, however remotely, might well prove fatal to the girl's bright hopes. And Joanna was very dear to her. It was all too easy for scandal to take root and flourish vigorously in the hot dusty days of the season's end. People were tired. Some were disappointed; others depressed as they discovered the extent of their bills. Few were in the mood to take a kindly and tolerant view of the peccadilloes of others. And if the notorious Miss Ingram, Queen of the Ton, should slip from grace, there would be many to delight in the fall, even if only as a distraction from their own troubles.

She had been so careful, too. To be honest, she had no inclination to be otherwise. A certain reserve was natural to her and she felt that the rules which governed the conduct of gently-bred young ladies were sensible and right. Not for her the clandestine visit to vulgar pleasure gardens or the secret assignation. And this season, with Joanna to think of, she had restrained even her natural friendliness, especially where gentlemen were concerned. Yet despite all her care, scandal had come perilously close. Two of her youngest admirers–a pair of callow young ensigns, neither of them above seventeen and admiring her only because she was the fashion, she thought indignantly–had indulged their high spirits in a ridiculous squabble about a rose which had fallen from her bouquet, the one claiming that she had dropped it deliberately for *him*, the other vowing–with perfect truth–that Miss Ingram would never award her favours so cheaply. They had been within ames ace of fighting over it. Only the blessed chance that their commanding officer was betrothed to Barbara Mansfield, and that Barbara, good sensible girl that she was, had lost no time in apprising him of the whole circumstances, had prevented a duel. The aspiring Lancelots had soon been set to rights. If they were so anxious to let each other's blood, they could do it with their fists. But to be bandying a lady's name about so freely, and she as far above them as the queen herself, was no behaviour for officers and gentlemen. Russet need fear no more trouble from that precious pair, he had told her comfortably.

But to come so close to disaster—and only for a fallen rose! Small wonder that she was anxious. She even had a slight headache, a discomfort that she rarely suffered. Joanna had driven into the country with Gilbert, duly chaperoned by Cousin Olivia. She would summon Agnes and stroll in the park. Perhaps the fresh air would mend her headache and surely nothing could go wrong on so innocuous an outing.

But as usual her strolling progress was continually interrupted by meetings with various other fashionables and she grew so weary of exchanging polite inanities that she had begun to wish herself back at home when a phaeton drawn by four splendid matched bays passed her and drew to a decorous halt a short distance down the track. It was sufficiently unusual to attract her attention. Most people considered two horses sufficient for so light a vehicle. But there was nothing ostentatious about the turn-out and the team was being handled with consummate skill. Russet was so absorbed in admiration of the horses that she did not at first notice that the gentleman who had climbed down from the seat beside the driver was trying to attract her attention. She glanced up enquiringly as he bowed and addressed her by name and then recognised a friend of Cousin Olivia's. She did not know him very well for he was a good deal older than her particular circle and something of a recluse into the bargain, with a reputation for being very knowledgeable about ancient civilisations; but she replied courteously to his enquiries about Cousin Olivia's health and assented politely when he asked if he might present Mr Cameron. She did not immediately associate the name with Letty Waydene's guardian and having duly acknowledged the introduction with a slight curtsey, expressed her admiration of the beautiful horses. Mr Cameron gravely begged her to do him the honour of taking a turn or two round the park, so that she could see for herself that their manners and paces matched their looks. To refuse would be ungracious. She bade Agnes wait for her and permitted herself to be handed up into the high-perched vehicle.

She was given little time to enjoy the drive. Mr Cameron had scarcely set his team in motion before he said abruptly, "I will confess at once, Miss Ingram, that I have been seeking an opportunity to speak to you in private for some time."

Under normal circumstances this frank approach would probably have appealed to her. In her present anxious mood she was instantly wary.

"In what way may I be of service to you, sir?" she said coldly.

"I believe that you are acquainted with my ward, Letty Waydene."

So that was it. Letty Waydene. And the need to calm and advise Lucian Staneborough had been not the least of her problems these past weeks. Only yesterday Letty had put her pretty little nose in the air and pretended not to see Russet when they had run smash into each other in Bond Street. Exasperation betrayed her into embittered speech.

"Acquaintance is too grand a term, sir, for something that Miss Waydene does not choose to recognise. It would be more accurate to say that she was a pupil at the academy where I was a junior governess."

Mr Cameron was surprised. He had expected her to be more artificial, more devious. He was not sure that he cared for such bluntness in a woman. He said slowly, "She is very unhappy."

If only he had stopped at that point! He chose instead to add, "And though I am sorry to say it, *you* are the principle cause of her unhappiness."

At this injustice all softer feelings vanished. She said icily, "I think you must explain yourself a little more clearly, sir."

So the wench thought to carry it with the high hand, did she? He dropped the mask of courtesy. "Do you deny that you have seduced her betrothed husband from his allegiance?" he shot at her. "All the world knows that Staneborough lives in your pocket. Even I, who live retired, have seen you weaving your spells. Why? Do you mean to marry him yourself? If that were so, almost I could forgive you. But it is no such thing. Idle, useless society dolls such as Miss Ingram must seek some new sensation to spice the boredom of a futile existence. You play these malicious games just for your entertainment, regardless of the hearts that you break, the sorrow that you bring. And to think that once you were considered a fit person to instruct the young! You should think shame to yourself."

He stopped short, horrified to hear himself descending to cheap melodramatics—and promptly blamed Miss Ingram. She did not *look* like a heartless siren. Unaccustomed to the ways of women, it was natural to him to think of her in terms of the horses that were his sole love. She had all the appearance of a high-bred filly, full of fire and spirit but never a particle of vice. It was the inconsistency between appearance and character that disturbed his judgement and led him to berate her so. He shut his lips firmly, resolved not to fall into error again. But the damage was done.

"Then permit me to tell you, sir," returned Miss Ingram in tones of searing fury, "that your ward has only her own petty jealousy to blame for her troubles. Mr Staneborough is certainly a gentleman whose friendship I am proud to claim. But he does not live in my pocket, nor is he likely to propose marriage to one whom he regards rather as a wise mama than as a girl of his own age. As for my conduct in the matter, it is, I believe, my own concern, so pray keep your strictures for your wards, who might possibly benefit from them. And here is Agnes patiently awaiting me," she added in a much more moderate key.

Since Agnes had already approached within earshot he was obliged to accept her departure. But if she thought that was the end of the matter, he thought grimly, she would learn better. Despite her denial it seemed pretty obvious that she meant to take Staneborough if she could get him up to scratch. She should discover that one James Cameron would have something to say to that. Nor was his sudden resolution solely on Letty's account. He had never been so thoroughly snubbed in his life and before he was done with her he would teach Miss Ingram a sharp lesson. Revolving the various ways in which this could be achieved he drove back to Cavendish Square, mentally adding a further score to Miss Ingram's account as he recalled all the afternoons that he had wasted in trying to achieve his end by diplomacy. Yes. Very definitely the time had come for sterner measures.

By the end of a week he had found out a good deal about Miss Ingram's circumstances. There were one or two points that he found a little puzzling since they did not fit his picture of the lady's character, but these he dismissed as unimportant. It was annoying, though, that she seemed to be quite invulnerable. He could discover nothing to her discredit that might have served as a weapon to force her into submission. Blackmail had a nasty ring to it but Mr Cameron had at least the honesty to acknowledge that this was what he had in mind. He consoled himself with the thought that Miss Ingram thoroughly deserved the punishment that was coming to her. But the devil was in it that he could not hit upon a suitable weapon. The lady's only reported weakness was her devotion to her sister, and not even Mr Cameron could see how that might be made to serve his purpose.

In the course of his extremely thorough investigations it was natural that Miss Ingram should be much in his mind. He went over their one conversation time and again. Here, also, there were inconsistencies. Miss Ingram appeared to think that her advanced age was the only thing that was holding Staneborough back. Mr Cameron had seen her at close quarters and in full sunlight, and he would not himself have thought—But no matter for that. He finally reached the conclusion that the girl must be a consummate actress. If he had not known from Letty of her perfidy, had not himself heard that brief snatch of conversation, he would have believed her to be honest in her indignation at his charge. Or perhaps she really was in love with Staneborough. That would explain conduct which, by all reports, was distinctly out of character.

Before he had time to reflect further along these lines, Letty made her next move. Three weeks had now elapsed since her first appeal to her guardian and she was growing impatient. She knew all about those afternoon drives in the park—such a departure from established practice had caused much comment. She even knew that on at least one occasion Miss Ingram had been her guardian's companion. She naturally assumed that he was following her suggestion and doing his best to divert the lady's attentions. Only he did not seem to be making much progress. It was time to apply the spur. She therefore told him in faltering tones that Lucian had offered to accompany Miss Ingram to Italy when she left to pay her annual visit to her Papa. No lady, he had said, should attempt so long and perilous a journey without the services of a courier to provide for her comfort and safety. Naturally she did not explain that the suggestion had been made in jest, with no thought of its being accepted, nor that it had been promptly laughed out of court by Miss Ingram with a brisk account of the number of times that she had made that same journey accompanied only by her sister, their maid and an experienced coachman, and of the ways in which they had dealt quite adequately with the various mishaps that are the general lot of travellers. Moreover she definitely tampered with the truth when she told him that Miss Ingram had said it would be time enough to think of couriers when she had found a respectable abigail to attend her on the journey, since on this occasion she meant to travel post and without her own devoted Agnes who was to accompany her sister on a visit to friends in the country. She was not, decided Letty virtuously, actually deceiving her guardian, since all the facts that she had stated were true, even if they had not, as she implied, been related in one conversation.

Mr Cameron could not at first understand why this shocking tale should have driven him into a towering rage. Miss Ingram's moral standards were really no concern of his. When he had simmered down a little he decided that it was because it represented a guerdon flung down to himself. He had dared to interfere. Very well, the chit had thought. Let him see what I can do if I really exert myself. She had probably engineered the whole, so that it should occur before the eyes of the innocent Letty and so, inevitably, be reported back to him.

Letty, who had seen the anger in his eyes, accepted brusque dismissal thankfully enough. Mr Cameron, possibly feeling that exercise, fresh air and a change of scene might dissipate his evil humour, ordered his travelling chaise to be brought round in an hour's time and left Town for a brief visit to his Hampshire estate.

Chapter Four

"I think that really *is* everything," decided Russet, with a rueful twinkle for her own fussing. "And you will not expect to hear from me for a month at least. I shall not write to you until I am safely installed at the villa and then we must allow for possible delays in the mail. But perhaps I had best address my letter to you at Denholme—in case you are invited to prolong your stay." And she smiled teasingly as Gilbert grinned and Joanna blushed as she settled back into her seat beside Agnes. Gilbert swung into the saddle and Russet waved the little party away with mixed feelings.

Predominant was relief that nothing had occurred at the last moment to cause any hitch in rather complicated arrangements. Cousin Olivia had departed on the previous day to stay with an old school friend in Wales, vowing that she would positively dote on rural isolation after all the bustle and noise of Town.

They had brushed through the last wearisome days of the season in tolerable comfort, and now Joanna was on her way to Denholme. So far, so good.

For Joanna's sake she prayed for a happy outcome, though she could not quite banish the reflection that her sister's marriage would leave her very lonely. While she was in Italy, she decided, she must devote some thought to devising a suitable occupation for the years ahead.

Meanwhile her own problems had resolved themselves with an almost miraculous simplicity. The abigail whom she had eventually engaged to go with her to Rome promised to be a real treasure. She was skilled in all the duties of her position though she confessed to ignorance of fashion's latest quirks, her last employer having been an elderly lady who had lost interest in such details. Russet did not mind that. Far more important was Phoebe's placid good sense. She had no objection to foreign travel; had, indeed, travelled widely, both on the continent and further afield, and made nothing of a mere journey to Rome. Even Agnes was prepared to give a qualified approval to her substitute, largely because Phoebe had shown herself willing to learn of her all about Miss Russet's particular likes and dislikes and had listened with grave respect to Agnes's pronouncements on this head.

In the matter of a carriage, too, she had been singularly fortunate. She had not been very happy at the prospect of using hired vehicles for so long a journey. Always before they had taken the carriage with their own familiar reliable coachman and one of the young grooms to share the task of driving. This year Russet had felt that Joanna must have prior claim on these amenities yet it seemed foolishly extravagant to buy another carriage for which she would have little use when her holiday was over. The owner of the livery stable which had supplied Cousin Olivia's postchaise had suggested a helpful alternative. He had just purchased a travelling chariot for his establishment. It was not new. A lady recently deceased had bequeathed it to her coachman. But it had been very carefully maintained and was both elegant and comfortable. If Miss Ingram would care to hire it for the duration of her holiday he thought he could persuade the coachman, a steady sort of man in his early forties, to undertake to drive it for her. The man was accustomed to good service and she could take one of her own grooms–or one of *his* lads if she preferred–and enjoy the degree of comfort to which she was accustomed.

When Russet inspected the chariot her mind was made up at once. It bore no resemblance to the usual type of vehicle offered for hire. Inside and out it gleamed with cleanliness, and though its leather lining was black and the curtains and carpeting a dark purple, colours too sombre for Russet's taste, it was every bit as comfortable as her own coach. The coachman, too, made a good impression. He could not, obviously, produce a reference from his last place, but he offered a bundle of testimonials affirming his sobriety and reliability that covered a period of twenty two years, and said that if Miss Ingram chose to enquire of his late employer's attorneys he was sure that they would vouch for him. She concluded the bargain forthwith, deciding to employ one of the lads from the livery stable rather than put a strange coachman over one of her own grooms for so short a period, and felt that she could now look forward to her journey with an easy mind.

She spent three leisurely days in completing her preparations for the holiday, indulging in one or two dawdling shopping expeditions to purchase such cool lawns and muslins as would be suitable to high summer in Italy. Phoebe accompanied her on these forays and proved herself so sensible and companionable that Russet began to consider the possibility of adding this excellent female to the household on a permanent footing. It made life even pleasanter when Herrick, the temporary coachman, was discovered to be known to Phoebe. At one time they had both served in the household of the same lady of quality—a countess, whose exact title escaped Russet's quick ear though it sounded foreign. It was of no particular consequence any way. What mattered was that the pair seemed to get on pretty well together which promised comfortable harmony for the protracted journey. Russet even pondered the possibility of fostering a romance between them, then decided that she should be ashamed to be contemplating such interference in the lives of others, even if only in private and for her own amusement, and turned her thoughts instead to the ordering of her journey.

Southampton was within a day's drive, but why hurry? She was more tired than she had thought. Better to lie overnight at Petersfield. That would allow an early arrival in Southampton with ample time for the loading of the carriage, always a long and complicated business though Herrick, she surmised, was probably quite as competent as their own faithful Tom coachman.

The drive to Petersfield went far to confirm this assumption. Herrick proved himself an able whip and his knowledge of the roads was superior—a fact that he discounted in pleasant fashion by saying that he had lived and worked in these parts for much of his life. He was able to suggest by-roads that were perfectly sound and well maintained yet quiet and pleasant.

Russet's night in Petersfield was peaceful, in the knowledge that her journey was in capable hands. She ventured the hope that fate had decided to smile on the Ingrams and that Joanna was equally favoured.

Next day, however, she was a trifle doubtful as to the wisdom of Herrick's choice of road for the run from Petersfield to Southampton. It was certainly very pretty but it was also very narrow. In places the overhanging hedges actually brushed the gleaming panels of the coach and she could not help wondering how it would be if they met another vehicle travelling at speed in one of these narrow places. But Herrick seemed quite unruffled and he could, of course, see much further ahead than she could from his lofty position on the box. She sat back in her corner, lowered the window and gave herself to enjoyment of the rural scene and the pleasant scents of new hay and honeysuckle that drifted in to her. The carriage was beautifully sprung and the narrowness of the road imposed a curb on the speed. So pleasant was the motion that Russet felt quite drowsy. Which was possibly the reason why she could not afterwards remember just how the accident occurred. At one moment they were jogging peacefully along the lane. At the next the carriage swerved violently and came to an abrupt, rocking halt, the body tilting perilously as the nearside wheels sank deeper into the ditch. Phoebe was flung unceremoniously on top of her mistress. Over the abigail's shoulder Russet caught a brief glimpse of a pair of powerful chestnuts harnessed to some light vehicle; of a spare, erect figure driving; and had the ridiculous notion that the three of them were flying, so swiftly did they flash past. By the time that she and Phoebe, with considerable difficulty because of the steep angle at which the carriage had come to rest, managed to extricate themselves from their corner, Herrick was tugging open the offside door, his voice raised in anxious enquiry, and the vehicle which had caused the accident had vanished, horses, driver and all, so completely that Russet blinked startled eyes and wondered if she had imagined it.

Herrick's remarks, however, once he was reassured as to the safety of his passengers, left her in no doubts on this score. "Went past us at a full gallop, he did, and never swerved by so much as a hair's breadth," he ejaculated. And then, rather surprisingly, "And never so much as a scratch on the paint. If I hadn't seen it for myself I'd not have believed it."

Russet looked at him curiously. He sounded almost admiring rather than properly furious. Perhaps the expression on her face served to remind him that his concern should be for his employer rather than for the paintwork of the carriage. There was apology in his voice as he said, "I'll need to go for help, ma'am. The horses ain't injured but it's more than they can manage to pull us out of the ditch, so deep as it is. There's a gentleman's house just round the next bend. Let me take you and Phoebe there where you can be comfortable, and maybe they'll be able to lend us farm horses and ropes. Smithers can stay with the horses."

Russet did not greatly care for the plan, not wishing to be beholden to a stranger, but she could hardly stand in the road for two or three hours and further enquiry discovered that the nearest posting inn was five miles away. Since Herrick now seemed sincerely concerned for her comfort she did not like to take him to task, though she thought it had been foolish to stray so far from frequented roads. It seemed best to fall in with his suggestion, and since Phoebe, too, apparently regarded casting oneself upon the charity of strangers as a very normal occurrence, Russet straightened her bonnet, shook out her skirts and followed her guide to a pair of handsome wrought iron gates that gave access to a well-kept park. No glimpse of the house could be seen from this approach but Herrick assured her that it was not very far, and was only invisible from this angle because of the sheltering trees, an assurance for which Russet could only be grateful. She had suffered no actual injury in the accident but now, she noticed with painful concentration, her hands and her knees were trembling uncontrollably and the hospitably open gates seemed to be wavering in a kind of haze. She had never fainted in her life but instinctively her hands went out to clutch at the graceful scrollwork. Dimly she heard Phoebe say sharply, "Catch her, Matt. She's going to faint. And no wonder, poor little lass. A cruel trick if ever I saw one."

Through the engulfing mists that threatened to overwhelm her, Russet felt sturdy arms catch and lift her; heard Herrick's voice reply gruffly, "Aye. But it had to be done and you know it. And maybe this way's best. There'll be no outcry. I'll carry her up without more ado—and she's taken no real hurt," he ended on a vaguely placatory note.

Even in her near senseless state Russet was aware of something desperately wrong. She struggled feebly in the coachman's hold, heard Phoebe say soothingly, "There now, dearie. Don't you fret. No harm shall come to you or my name's not Phoebe Herrick," and was again aware that these would-be comforting words posed yet another mysterious threat. It was her last conscious thought.

She came up from the depths to a fleeting sense of security and warmth. Someone had taken off her dress and shoes and loosened her stay-laces. Phoebe's motherly arms were supporting her as she lay stretched on a day-bed,

Phoebe's voice encouraged her to swallow a bitter tasting potion that was held to her lips, assuring her that she would feel very much more the thing when she had done so. She drank obediently. The draught certainly seemed to dispel some of the wavering blending outlines that still made her feel giddy, but she was shivering convulsively and feared that she might yet be sick if she did not lie still with her eyes closed until natural objects resolved themselves into their own distinctive shapes once more. Someone was gently chafing her icy feet and she could feel the gentle warmth that was gradually returning to her limbs as a result of these ministrations. She wanted to voice her thanks for such kindness and opened her eyes as she tried to express her gratitude. The girl who was kneeling at the foot of the day-bed glanced up. From beneath the shelter of a rose-coloured sari a pair of huge brown eyes timidly returned her gaze. Russet had never before seen a Hindu maiden but even in her half-waking, half-dreaming state she recognised that this was no ordinary abigail. Her mouth trembled into a rather shaky smile. She overcame the drowsiness that seemed to be creeping over her for just long enough to whisper a shy, "Thank you–you are very"–and the heavy lids closed again as she succumbed to the powerful sleeping draught that she had swallowed.

It was evening before she roused. She lay passive for a while, still half stupid from the effect of the drug, puzzling as to what she was doing lying in this very comfortable bed in a perfectly strange room. Phoebe was sitting in a low rocking chair in the window, her needles clicking softly as she knitted and crooned a mournful little air, but somehow Russet did not think that this was the bedchamber that had been reserved for her at the Dolphin where she had expected to lie tonight. Certainly it did not look like any room that she had ever previously occupied in an inn. In fact there was an air of luxury that was unusual even in a private house. The quilt on which her fingers rested was of heavy satin, richly embroidered in glowing silks and the room itself was furnished rather as a sitting room than a bedroom, with a sewing table drawn up to the hearth and shelves of books filling half of one wall.

But Russet could not surrender to the beguiling atmosphere of comfort. Troubling memories were pricking her to an anxious wakefulness. The accident to the carriage; it had seemed, at the time, just one of the chances of the road. One took the risk of encounters with such reckless selfishness whenever one travelled. But it *was* unusual that the erring driver of those chestnuts had not stopped to assure himself that no real damage had been done. What gave her further cause for concern was that half-heard, half-remembered conversation between her two attendants. She lay with closed eyes trying to recall it more precisely. There had been something about a cruel trick, with Phoebe indignant and Herrick saying it was better so because there would be no outcry. And yes! That was it! Phoebe had referred to herself as Phoebe Herrick. Yet Russet had engaged her as Phoebe Gilbey. The small circumstance was capable of an innocent interpretation of course, but taken in conjunction with the other disturbing remarks that were coming back to her it seemed most probable that for some inexplicable reason she had been cozened and deceived.

Summoning all her determination she struggled up on to one elbow, though even that slight exertion made her feel sick and giddy. At the sound of movement Phoebe glanced across at her, put down her work and picked up a glass that stood on a stool by the sewing table.

"Drink this, miss," she said quietly. "You'll be feeling sick as a cushion I doubt, but this'll soon put you to rights."

Russet pushed the proffered glass aside. "No thank you," she said, with as much dignity as trembling lips and a distinctly wobbly voice would permit. "I distrust your draughts—Miss Herrick. Or is it Mrs Herrick?"

Discovery did not seem to cause Phoebe any vast embarrassment. "Matt said he reckoned as how you'd heard me," she said composedly, "and that you'd be quick to ferret out the whole. I never was much of a one for play acting. Not that it matters, now. And though you'll not believe me, it's downright sorry I was that we had to treat you so. What's more, though I'd not try to force you, this"—she indicated the glass—"really will make you feel more the thing."

Despite all the evidence of the woman's duplicity there was something in face and voice that carried conviction. Russet stared at her for a long, measuring moment, and put out her hand for the glass. Phoebe actually coloured up, so pleased she was, and came to plump up the pillows behind her as she sipped. And her trust was justified. Whatever was in the glass, it had an excellent restorative effect. Presently she was able to sit erect and gaze about her. Her first fleeting impression of the room in which she lay was amply confirmed. The furnishings were perhaps a little too opulent for *her* taste. Costly and elegant though they were, they conveyed an impression of heaviness that might, in time, become stifling. Russet would have exchanged the rich damasks for lighter fabrics, the vast four-poster in which she lay for a simple tent-bed. She drank slowly and studied her surroundings with a determinedly critical eye, instinctively deferring the frightening moment when she must ask for an explanation of all this mystery. Though the business had been conducted without violence, save for that skilfully contrived 'accident' she had small doubt that she had been abducted. Presumably for ransom, though one would scarcely have supposed the owner of all this lavish display to have any need of replenishing his coffers by such dubious methods.

She drained the glass and set it back on the stool, bracing herself to face whatever revelations lay in store with the fortitude expected of an Ingram. Phoebe plunged a hand into the pocket of her grey stuff gown and pulled out a letter which she tendered rather nervously. It was the first time that she had betrayed any agitation.

"It's a letter from the master, miss," she explained. "But don't be feared. He'd not hurt you. I'd never have lent myself to the business, not even for him, if I'd not had his word that no harm should come to you. And he's one that keeps his promises, even if he *is* a mite high-handed at times."

The exhortation was just what Russet needed to brace her quivering nerves. "Of course I'm not afraid," she said indignantly, small nose well in the air. "Afraid of a man who not only descends to the abduction of helpless females but gets servants to do his dirty work for him? No such thing, I promise you." And refused to acknowledge the relief that had flooded through her at Phoebe's reassurances. Odd how she still felt inclined to trust the woman after the way she had behaved, but so it was. She took the letter and opened it gingerly, rather as she might have handled a loaded pistol. Thick, expensive paper and a forceful rather than elegant superscription.

No time wasted on unnecessary courtesies, either. Perhaps one should not expect such refinements from a wretch so depraved as to stoop to one of the vilest crimes. It was just that her present surroundings conveyed the implication of culture and good manners. The letter began brusquely:

Madam,

It has become desirable that you be removed for a while from the social scene that you are accustomed to adorn.

You have no cause for alarm. Neither your person, your virtue nor your fortune stand in any danger. The worst that you will be called upon to endure is the boredom inseparable from a period of close confinement, and I have been at some pains to ensure that your prison shall be as comfortable as is consistent with security.

I regret that at this present I am unable to advise you as to how long your imprisonment must endure. Pray accept my assurance that you shall be released as soon as the problem that you have created has been satisfactorily solved.

James Cameron.

Russet read it once, hastily; flicked over the paper to stare at the signature sprawled across the second sheet, and raised a face in which rage and sheer incredulity fought a drawn battle. The arrogance! The downright insolence of daring to put his name to such a document! Did he not know that the penalty for abduction was transportation at the very least? Yet he had supplied her with tangible evidence of his guilt as carelessly as though it was of no consequence at all.

She perused the missive again. It certainly sorted well with what she knew of the man. In their one encounter he had been just as blunt. One must allow him a certain sort of honesty, she decided reluctantly. A pity that it was not used to better purpose. There seemed to be little doubt that she owed her present undignified situation to Letty Waydene's machinations. She wondered what lies Letty had told her guardian to drive him to such rash action, and then, furiously, whether the girl knew what he had done. Somehow that possibility seemed to her the one insupportable feature of a humiliating position. There were storm signals flying in her cheeks, a militant sparkle in the hazel eyes as she said steadily, "You may dress me. I will see Mr Cameron."

Phoebe actually looked flustered. "But you can't do that, miss," she protested.

"Why not?" demanded Russet, her head thrown back, every inch an Ingram. "Since he is in some sort my host I must naturally pay him all such attentions as are his due."

And now there was frank admiration in Phoebe's eye. She had taken a marked fancy to Miss Ingram at their first meeting and it was satisfying to have that liking confirmed. A lass of pluck and spirit. No megrims, no useless bewailings. She would carry battle to the enemy. Almost, thought Phoebe, she might have proved herself a match for Mr James. But of course all the advantages were on his side. The girl was fast prisoned and there could be no escape. She said submissively, "The master is away from home tonight, miss."

Russet did not know whether to be grateful for the respite or not. To be sure she was not feeling quite herself, still shaken from her unpleasant experiences. But it might have been better to have the necessary encounter over and done with while righteous anger still sustained her spirits. She said, as one sadly shocked and disappointed, "Dear me! How very remiss! So much trouble as he has taken to persuade me to accept his hospitality, I had certainly expected a personal welcome.

But I suppose," she added reflectively, "that one should not ask too much of people of mixed blood. Mongrel curs are notoriously unreliable."

Phoebe looked frightened. Her rosy country complexion paled. "Miss," she faltered urgently. "Never say such a thing to the master, I beg of you. Proud as Lucifer he is, both of his Scottish blood and of his mother's. Seems she was as near royalty as makes no difference in those outlandish parts." Her fingers flew up to her mouth in dismay. "Only outlandish to the likes of me, because I'm ignorant," she said defensively. "There's no denying she was a proper lady through and through, as I should know that served her twenty years and more. *And* a royal way with her when it came to generosity and remembering them that had helped her in adversity. For poor she had been—aye, even gone hungry, times, when she was young. What matters more is that Mr James just about worshipped her. If you was to say a word that reflected on his mama he'd go mad. And then there's no saying what he'd do, for in his black moods he can be merciless."

Russet was impressed despite herself. It was clear that Phoebe, at any rate, fully believed what she had said and that her warning was given out of concern for Russet's well-being. She remembered that she was a prisoner in the hands of this unpredictable creature. It might be diplomatic to tread warily, however much the necessity irked her. Besides, her quarrel was not with Mr Cameron's mother. Perhaps, after all, it was as well that she need not meet him tonight. By tomorrow she would be rested and refreshed, more able to assess the situation and deal wisely with her captor. But it would not do to confess this relief. Phoebe, however sympathetic her attitude, was in the enemy camp.

"In that case I will have dinner served to me here," she announced regally. "And pray see to it that it is none of your invalid messes—unless your master has decided to starve me into submission. I am perfectly well and in good appetite. And a glass of wine, I think. It seems that I may have need of all my strength."

And Phoebe, turning away to conceal her appreciative grin for such mettle, went to give the required order.

Chapter Five

"But you cannot seriously mean to keep me shut up here indefinitely for so ridiculous a reason! One, moreover, which is wholly without foundation save in your imagination—or possibly in Miss Waydene's."

He shrugged, slender hands spread eloquently in a gesture that indicated amusement barely concealed by the mask of courtesy. "One naturally hesitates to contradict a lady," he bowed politely.

She took his meaning. "Do you imagine that I shall not be missed?" she said indignantly. "I daresay the search is already on, since I failed to arrive at the Dolphin last night."

"Well as to that," he said smoothly—and one might almost have thought him sincerely apologetic—"I took the liberty of cancelling the rooms that you had engaged. You must not be blaming Mr Neal. He knows me pretty well, you see, since I always use the Dolphin when I have cause to stay in Southampton, and since I told him a plausible tale about your arrangements being changed at the last moment because of a pressing invitation to stay with friends he had no cause to disbelieve me. Especially as I also told him that you insisted on paying for the rooms since it was such short notice."

But Russet had herself well in hand. "You may be able to bribe such people as inn servants and livery stablemen," she told him in a voice that matched his own for cool indifference, "but I have relatives and friends who will not prove so gullible. How do you propose to deal with their enquiries when I am found to be missing?"

A faint smile curved the firm mouth. "I am afraid that you will not quite like it. But if you insist I am perfectly willing to explain my plan."

She did not deign to reply to this, contenting herself with tapping one small foot impatiently and composing her features into what she hoped was an expression of impersonal interest.

"Perhaps I should first explain that I am a little acquainted with your Papa," began her tormentor. "Not intimately, of course, since he is so much the older, but sufficiently, I believe, to be able to estimate his thoughts and his reactions with reasonable accuracy. Do you really rely on his causing enquiry to be made for you? To start with it will be a fortnight at least before he even notices your non-arrival. Then he will decide that he must have mistaken the date—perhaps even the month—of your coming. He may look for the last letter that you wrote him, announcing your plans, but will be unable to find it, having used it to write down the name of a fancied horse or the address of a snug little gaming house. More simply he may just assume that you have been delayed by one of the many slight mishaps which befall travellers. Parental concern may lead him to mild excesses by way of distracting his mind. I do not think it will cause him to set any serious enquiry on foot."

For the first time Russet knew fear. The pleasant, dispassionate voice detailing her parent's all too probable reactions to her disappearance was far more frightening than bluster or threats because it bore the very stamp of truth. Her father *was* of just such an easy-going and optimistic temperament as would cause him to delay action in the happy confidence that she was bound to turn up safely sooner or later. Mr Cameron's words indicated a knowledge of her affairs that was far too accurate for comfort, and a ruthless determination to use it.

Worse was to follow. "After our first abortive encounter," the deep, soft voice went on,

"I made it my business to find out all that I could about you and your family. It seemed to me that the knowledge might prove useful in the event of your continued refusal to behave reasonably. So, indeed, it proved." He smiled, and said reflectively, "If I had dealt the cards myself I could not have chosen a better hand. Consider. Your chaperone cousin has gone off to the heart of rural Wales. I doubt if they have even heard of a mail service in those parts. Certainly she will not expect to hear from you for a month at least, and probably will not worry unduly over an even longer delay. Your sister—ah! Here we come to the nub of the matter. Naturally she will not expect to hear from you until you have had ample time to complete your journey. A few more days she may well ascribe to delays in the mail. But if popular opinion is correct in reporting that you are sincerely attached to each other, she will begin to fret if she does not hear from you within, let us say, a month. And that despite her preoccupation with her own affairs."

He pronounced those last words slowly and thoughtfully. Russet maintained a brave front but her heart quailed. This man knew it all. Knew all about Joanna's visit and how much might hang upon its success. In this one spot she was vulnerable indeed. But she was proud, too. And Joanna would be the first to insist that she should not yield to blackmail. Somehow she would win free of her captivity, foil this horrid wretch who was so smugly pleased with his own cleverness before Joanna had time to grow anxious for her.

He said gently, "I think I may safely reckon that by the time any serious search is instituted, you will have been in my hands for a month or more. I wonder how the Denholmes will regard such an escapade? For my part I cannot feel that it will add to the pleasure with which they will welcome your sister into their family."

The pretty colour bestowed by anger faded. The girl looked as though she might swoon, and the great golden eyes looked at him in dumb appeal as might some hunted hind's. But his first duty was to Letty and it would be folly to allow pity to soften his attitude now when a little firmness might gain him what he wanted. Mr Cameron folded his arms and waited with all the appearance of a heartless jailer.

The girl said quietly, "Surely your quarrel is with me. Not with my sister who has certainly never injured you in any way."

He smiled; and Russet thought she had never seen so cruel and cold a face. "But you, my dear, are only vulnerable through your sister. I assure you that I wish the pretty creature no harm. Denholme may wed her with my very good will. But first she shall serve her purpose by bending you to my wishes."

"And they are?"

He studied her thoughtfully. "At first," he said slowly, "I had some notion of exacting a solemn promise from you that in future you would let Staneborough alone. But it will not serve. What reason have I to accept your word? Once free you could laugh at me; could say, with some reason, that promises extracted by force are not binding. Some safeguard stronger than a mere promise is needed."

Just for a moment she fancied that a hint of embarrassment showed in the saturnine countenance. Then, as one embarking on a carefully rehearsed speech, he said, "Though I myself am a bachelor, I have considerable faith in the matrimonial tie as the one best fitted to control the behaviour of foolish and headstrong young women. I have decided that it would be better for you to marry."

Russet forgot all about keeping a cool impassive countenance in the face of the enemy. In the whole of her life she had never heard anything so astounding, or, indeed, so utterly absurd. Her mouth dropped open as she stared at him aghast. Surely, oh, surely he was not going to suggest that she should marry him! Yet that remark about being a bachelor seemed to presage some such incredible proposal. A new threat reared its ugly head. Was Mr Cameron quite sane?

Mr Cameron, however, having broached his fantastic scheme and allowed his prisoner time to consider its possibilities, proceeded to enlarge on it in a very businesslike way with no least inkling of that prisoner's horrified reaction.

"I am credibly informed," he went on, with the faintly distasteful air of one compelled to discuss a subject of doubtful propriety, "that you have any number of suitors. Several of whom are extremely eligible. So there can be no problem there. You have only to indicate which of them you prefer, and I will make all the necessary arrangements to inform the happy man of your decision."

But Russet had recovered. "For one who is so remarkably well informed and such a percipient judge of the possible reactions of others," she told him tartly, "you seem to have very little knowledge of the behaviour of the *normal* members of your sex." The slight stress that she gave to 'normal' was dangerous, she knew, but irresistible. "What do you think would be the feelings of the chosen gentleman—and there was no need to sneer at the number of my suitors—when informed by *you* that I had decided to marry *him*? Ignorant and unprincipled as I am, I can think of only one interpretation that he would put upon such a suggestion. And I do not think that it would be *marriage* that he would have in mind."

It was Mr Cameron's turn to look slightly non-plussed. But he was of a dogged breed that having once decided upon a course of action would not lightly be turned aside. "You have only to think of your sister's future," he said smoothly, "and I feel sure that feminine ingenuity will enable you to concoct a tale that will convince the fortunate gentleman of your unimpeachable virtue."

She eyed him with loathing. But for Joanna's sake she would make one more effort at conciliation, whatever the cost to her pride. "Why should it not suffice," she said meekly, "that I give you my word that I have no designs on Lucian Staneborough? At its very lowest level, surely your intimate knowledge of my–my suitors–must have indicated that I could do better for myself. And I have repeatedly assured you that the whole thing is a hum–that Lucian does not care for me in that way. Can you not accept my word for this?"

His face was grim. "Unfortunately, ma'am, no. Perhaps I might have done so had I not learned in Southampton last night that Staneborough had met with an accident upon his arrival in that town. No–it was not of my contriving," he threw in impatiently as he saw alarm and suspicion in her face, "nor was he seriously hurt. A broken ankle, I believe, and caused by sheer negligence, wandering about the quayside and not looking where he was going—so intent, no doubt, on seeking a certain Miss Ingram. But with matters in such a pass I am not going to accept empty promises. Moreover you could not, in any case, promise for Staneborough, could you? No. I'll see you safely tied up in matrimony, where you can do no more harm, or you may stay here. The choice is with you."

"There *is* no choice," she said curtly. "Not even for my sister's sake could I consent to so base a betrayal."

He seemed surprised. "You would deem it so?"

"To marry a man who had offered for me in honesty, just to suit my own convenience? Would not *you* call it betrayal? Or, indeed, to marry at all when my affections were not engaged. What sort of a bargain would that be? No, sir. I fear that you will be put to the trouble and expense of housing me for some considerable time."

She gave him a tiny curtsey to signify that the interview was now ended. But he was not yet quite done with her.

"Very well, ma'am. On the day that my ward's betrothal is officially announced, you will be free to go. I regret that such an announcement is likely to be further delayed by Staneborough's mishap. Perhaps I am over generous in my estimate of him, but once that announcement has been sent to the papers I do not think that he could be beguiled into breaking his troth. If, on the other hand, the tedium of imprisonment should cause you to change your mind on the subject of marriage, you have merely to acquaint me with your wishes. Ameera will bring me the message. She is to wait on you, and will supply you with all reasonable comforts. Anything short of freedom. You have only to ask."

This was another blow. "Ameera?" questioned Russet. "Not Phoebe?"

The grim face softened. "No. Not Phoebe. Phoebe is my housekeeper. It was quite sufficiently uncomfortable having to dispense with her services for a whole week. I cannot spare her to you for longer. Besides, she disapproves of my present course of conduct and has not scrupled to tell me so. You might find it possible to work on her sympathies to a point where she would connive at your escape. You will not be able to do that with Ameera since her command of English is limited. She is, however, well trained in the duties required of a lady's maid, so her linguistic shortcomings are unimportant. Incidentally, although she looks slight and frail, do not try to wrest the key of your room from her. You might well succeed in doing so. But Ameera herself is locked in with you. This room, with the adjoining dressing room, is approached by a separate corridor. The door to that corridor is locked and bolted on the outside by my butler, Ahmed Khan, Ameera's father, so all that you would gain by such an attempt is the freedom of that corridor and the hostility of my Indian servants. I will leave you to think things over and bid you good morning."

But Russet was in no mood for careful reflection. Her spirits had sunk at the knowledge that she was to be deprived of Phoebe's society. It seemed that she had been right in her instinctive trust. Phoebe *did* symphathise with her, even though loyalty to her master had led to her being involved in the abduction. With Phoebe to turn to, Russet could have felt safe and comfortable, even if she was a prisoner. Deprived of that support she felt oddly helpless and very lonely. She would have liked to bury her face in the cushions of the window seat where she had established herself and give way to the misery that was making the tears prick behind her eyelids and her throat ache with suppressed sobs. But that was no way for an Ingram to behave, and who knew when the soft-footed Ameera might choose to appear? It would never do to be discovered giving way to despair, since doubtless a report would promptly go back to her jailer.

Instead she began, like every other captive creature, to probe the boundaries of her prison.

It did not take very long, and so far as she could see there was no possibility of escape. The two rooms together made the shape of an L and formed one corner of the building. The dressing room had only a small casement window which looked out over sloping lawns to a lake and the graceful trees of the park. What looked like another door out of it gave access only to a powder closet. The bedroom, which overlooked what Russet guessed to be the main drive, had three large sash windows, one of which actually stood open. But since investigation revealed that the terrace was some thirty feet below, Russet soon abandoned any wild hope of knotting the bed sheets together and using this way of escape. To arrive on that remarkably unreceptive-looking terrace in a huddled heap, with broken limbs or possibly even a broken neck, could scarcely serve any useful purpose and would probably create just the kind of scandal that she was so anxious to avoid.

One small taste of liberty was granted her. A beautiful wrought iron balcony ran the length of the three windows, just such a balcony as she had once seen adorning a Venetian palace. It was furnished with tubs of plants, some of which had been trained to form a screen from the glare of the sun, and with chairs and a table of wicker-work. An Indian notion, perhaps, for she had never seen anything quite like them before. At least they seemed to show that the balcony was meant for use and that she need not fear to entrust herself to its support. She climbed carefully over the low window sill and advanced rather timidly to the balustrade. One glance at the terrace below was more than sufficient. She had never had much of a head for heights. Hastily she averted her gaze from that intimidating drop and its horrid fascination. It required quite a strong effort of will to ignore it and force herself to concentrate on the other aspects of her surroundings.

Along the frontage of the house were two more balconies that matched hers. She guessed that these probably served the principal bedrooms, while the floor below would be given over to reception rooms. Best not to think too much about the floors below, she decided. They reminded her of that drop. She wondered who had formerly used her room. Possibly Mr Cameron's mother, since the heavy furnishings seemed to indicate the preferences of an older woman. Though if the gentleman had held his mother in such esteem as Phoebe would have had her believe, he would surely not have given over her room to house a 'useless society doll'. *That* insult still rankled, perhaps because it held a certain element of truth. She *did* lead a useless existence; had herself wearied of it. But what else was a girl to do? At least she furnished useful employment for quite a number of other people who would otherwise have been without the means of subsistence.

She sighed wearily. What she had to do at this moment was to devise a way out of this impasse. And at least, she thought resentfully, if she was idle and useless, she was not wantonly wicked like Letty Waydene, whom his lordliness seemed to think so perfect and so ill-used. She did not tell malicious lies or harm innocent people. She wondered inconsequently how Joanna was getting on, and if Gilbert had declared himself as yet. They would have been at Denholme for two days now. The thought led her naturally to speculation about Lucian Staneborough. Because she liked the lad, she sincerely hoped that his injuries were minor ones, as Mr Cameron had seemed to imply. For her own sake, also, she wished him a speedy recovery. If he were to announce his betrothal to Letty without further delay, it would be much the simplest way out of her difficulties. It was a very selfish thought, she knew, for what hope of happiness could there be for a decent straightforward youngster, wedded to sly, scheming Miss Letty?

But for the moment she had troubles enough of her own. She was by nature an active energetic creature, and the beauty of the summer day seemed to mock her helplessness. A gentle breeze stirred the tree-tops. She thought how delightful it would be to walk or drive out on such a morning. Better still to ride. From the terrace below a peacock screeched, and strutted proudly, displaying his glorious train. No other living creature stirred.

She wearied soon enough of the balcony with its taunting illusion of freedom and turned to seek distraction indoors. She examined the shelves of books. Many of them were works of a religious or philosophical nature, but there were several volumes of poetry and a number of novels. As a rule Russet enjoyed reading but today she found it impossible to concentrate on the printed page. There was a handsome escritoire furnished with everything that a lady could desire if she wished to deal with her correspondence. And small use *that* was, she thought bitterly, unless she decided to keep a diary to record the days of her imprisonment. She was in no mood for needlework—was not, in any case, overfond of her needle—and had no aptitude for sketching in water colours. If the specimens on the walls were evidence, her predecessor had possessed marked talent. There were some charming studies of rural scenes showing sturdy peasants, vigorous with life, engaged in seasonal tasks. Not English, Russet decided, briefly interested. There was a slightly romanticised painting—in oils, this time, and on a sizeable canvas—of a hoary looking mediaeval castle complete with moat, drawbridge and a faint air of melancholy, as though it brooded over glories long faded. She would have liked to know more about the castle—its story might prove more interesting than any of the novels—and about the artist. But there was no one to ask. Whether from choice or because she had been so instructed, Ameera's visits were brief; no more than was necessary to attend to Russet's toilet and to serve her meals. Once another maid came with her to set the room to rights and Russet had to retire to the balcony while this was done, but the second girl never spoke at all though her big dark eyes were alight with eager curiosity. Perhaps *she* had *no* English. Ameera's, while perfectly adequate to the exigencies of a lady's toilet and to simple exchanges about meals, did not allow of anything more intimate.

A pack of playing cards, discovered in one of the drawers of the escritoire, helped a little. She occupied herself in dealing out hands for the players in various games and in trying to assess how the game would have gone. Between that and playing herself at chess the time passed somehow. At least her fingers were busy even if her thoughts were frequently astray.

There were two clocks to mark the passage of the hours. One, a charming Louis Quinze piece, stood on the mantel shelf. The other, a chiming clock of some kind, was presumably outside in the corridor. By dusk she would gladly have set about that one with a hammer. The mantel clock she could endure—one could always turn one's back on it. The other wretched brute—by now she had imbued it with a separate animate personality—insisted on reminding her that only another quarter of an hour had passed; that it was still two hours to dinner; that at least three more must be endured before one could decently retire to bed. Deeply she regretted that an Ingram could scarcely ask that the thing should be stopped. Tomorrow, perhaps, she thought hopefully. One could always say that it disturbed one's slumbers. But no. The excuse was too flimsy. *HE* would detect the subterfuge, and triumph over this sign of weakness.

She took what comfort she could from the delicious meals that were served to her. Not so much from the food itself—between anxiety and lack of exercise her appetite was already failing—but because she ascribed the daintily prepared trays, the provision of her favourite dishes, to Phoebe's kindly thought for her, and hugged that friendly warmth to her loneliness.

Chapter Six

If the first day of her captivity had seemed endless, those that followed merged into a monotonous sameness where time was of small importance. She found herself succumbing to a dull apathy, broken occasionally by fits of wild frustration. In these angry moods she even knew the urge to smash and destroy. She never saw Mr Cameron. Save for Ameera and the young housemaid no one came near her, and there were times when, since she could not get at her jailer to pour out her fury, she was sorely tempted to do all the damage she could, to spoil and deface this opulent prison that mocked her with its smug comfort. That she never did so was because she knew that it would be a moral victory for her tormentor.

From lack of exercise and occupation she slept badly, and the tempting meals that Phoebe caused to be sent up to her would often go back to the kitchen untouched. She grew pale and heavy-eyed, all of which the tender-hearted Ameera faithfully reported to a deeply concerned Phoebe.

After that first endless day she had taught herself to pursue a course of varied occupation, spending one hour on reading a volume of sermons, another sewing, a third in her endless foolish card games, meticulously recording the scores of Joanna or Cousin Olivia or some other chosen opponent. After lunch she would sit on the balcony with a novel. But not even the tragic fate of the lovely Clarissa Harlowe could wholly distract her mind. She would read the same paragraph over and over again without taking in its meaning and close the book with a sigh of relief when the clock struck the hour. What most alarmed Ameera was the trick she had developed of talking to herself. There were tears in the girl's eyes when for the third time she had to tell Phoebe of this strange behaviour.

"It is bad," she said sorrowfully. "Missy is kind and gentle. Why she be shut in? She grow ill."

"And talking to herself," muttered Phoebe anxiously. "The lonesomeness, poor little wench. And the master forbidding me to go next nor nigh her. Trying to tame her spirit and can't see that she's the kind that'll break before it yields. It'd not surprise me if he's not got hold of the wrong end of the stick. Miss

Russet didn't seem like no fast and loose piece to me, while that there Miss Letty was too smooth by half, with her pretty coaxing ways and her demure looks, and her as smug as a cat at the cream pot."

"Cat!" she said, so sharply and so suddenly that poor Ameera, who had been painstakingly trying to follow these idiomatic remarks, nearly jumped out of her skin. "Cats," she repeated, more calmly. "That'd be the thing. A kitten. T'would be company for her and give her something to talk to. *And* the master never said we wasn't to give her a kitten to play with," she ended triumphantly.

Alas! This promising scheme seemed doomed to failure for lack of suitable livestock. The kitchen cat, which, said Phoebe, produced litters with quite unnecessary regularity, was not due to oblige for another week. By the time her expected progeny were of an age to be introduced into parlours, Phoebe devoutly trusted that their unwilling guest would be safely restored to her own home. And even Phoebe was forced to admit that it would not do to be asking around the farms for a kitten suitable for a lady's pet. Such an unusual request would certainly provoke undesirable curiosity. They wanted no rumours of strange ladies staying at Furze House.

It was left to the delighted Ameera to

suggest an alternative. "Chimi!" she said. "The missy like Chimi."

Phoebe was dubious. "A monkey," she pondered. "Well, I don't know. Smart London ladies *do* have pet monkeys, I believe. But it's not a Christian kind of animal like a cat or a dog."

Ameera giggled. "Chimi no Christian," she said. "He very good Hindu. But he make the missy laugh."

At least the retort made Phoebe laugh, and Ameera was given permission to introduce her pet into Russet's room as soon as the master had gone out.

The diversion succeeded to admiration. Russet was interested and amused. Chimi's mischievous antics actually *did* make her laugh. He was an amiable little creature and enjoyed being petted, wrapping his skinny arms around her and chittering happily in the fashion that had given him his name. Russet fed him with cherries and nuts and smiled to see him spit nutshells and cherry stones on to the elegant day-bed and go swarming nonchalantly up the detested damask curtains. He was quite willing to stay with her, too, as long as the supply of food held out, and Ameera went off to her other duties well pleased with the success of her kindly thought, while Chimi, worn out by so much socialising, curled up on the day-bed and went to sleep.

A brief nap, however, soon restored him to his normal state of inquisitive activity, and having investigated the fruit bowl and found it empty he proceeded to explore further. He swung himself easily over the window sill and before Russet could stop him had climbed on to the verandah balustrade. Frantically she called his name, fearing that he would fall and be hurt, but he did not know her voice and preferred to remain on his airy perch. She looked around for something to tempt him back but there was nothing, unless he would fancy the sweetmeats that Ameera had shyly offered the other day and which still lay untouched in their dish on the escritoire. By the time that she had crossed the room and snatched up one of the sweet sticky morsels, the rascal had vanished. He was nowhere on the balcony, nowhere in the room. Her revulsion from the depths below was lost in sharp fear for Ameera's pet. She hung anxiously over the balustrade scanning the terrace. But blessedly there was no small pathetic bundle of bones and fur on the flagstones below. Could a monkey fall so far and escape unharmed? It was difficult to believe, but where else could he be?

Then she heard him chittering at her. He must have been hiding in the greenery all the time, but still she could not see him and stared about her in puzzled fashion until the indignant chittering drew her attention to the balcony of the room next door. The runaway was perched on the balcony rail with nonchalant ease, grinning at her coquettishly and eyeing with interest the sticky sweet that she was still holding. How he had got there was a monkey mystery but presumably he could come back safely enough if he so chose. Fortunately the windows behind him were closed so he was not tempted to stray further. While still she hesitated, uncertain whether it would be wise to try and coax him back, greed overcame his mischievous coyness. He swung easily over the balustrade, ran along a narrow ledge which connected the floors of the two balconies, and snatched the sweet from her fingers, retreating immediately to the top of the curtains where he devoured his trophy with glutinous enjoyment. Russet made haste to close the window and then, having supplied her greedy little guest with one more sweet, to cover the remainder lest he make himself sick and to wash her sticky fingers.

Ameera, bringing her lunch, was delighted to find her in better spirits. With the assistance of a certain amount of pantomime the monkey's addiction to sweets was explained. Ameera shook her head at him reprovingly but managed to assure Russet that his constitution was not permanently damaged. Next time—if Russet understood her aright—he should wear his collar, which made him much easier to catch. She then removed him, promising to bring him visiting again tomorrow.

Russet ate her lunch with improved appetite but pensively, wholly failing to appreciate the subtle perfection of the sauce served with the duckling, a sauce which the chef himself had prepared. Fortunately for domestic harmony at Furze House, she *did* eat it, thereby causing that devoted disciple of Epicurus to put on the most insufferable airs. She also, though absent-mindedly, drank the glass of claret that Phoebe's anxious hand had added to the collation. Possibly it was the wine that caused her to be more than usually impatient with Clarissa Harlowe. Her gaze strayed repeatedly from that tragic heroine's letters to the stone ledge that Chimi had negotiated with such ease. She wondered how it was that she had not noticed it before. It was clearly the foundation on which the balconies rested, and quite strong enough to support an escaping fugitive, but not the most optimistic scrutiny could make it wide enough for safety. Especially when that fugitive was admittedly afraid of heights. If only one could not *see* that daunting drop. Perhaps when it was dark? But that would make the crossing doubly dangerous. And unless there was a window left open in the adjoining room it would be useless any way. If she was a heroine in a book, she thought crossly, she would undoubtedly be both fearless and athletic; and concentrated resolutely on Clarissa.

But she could not help observing that the necessary windows were opened for a time each morning and evening. She was obliged to study them in case Chimi, now a regular daily visitor, should suddenly decide to effect an illegal entry by that route. Morning was hopeless. In full daylight she *could* not shut her eyes to the consequences of a fall, let alone the probability of being seen, clinging like a fly to a honey-comb, as she essayed the perilous passage. But evening–with kindly darkness blanketing those intimidating flagstones and a full moon giving light sufficient to permit avoidance of minor obstacles–might be a very different pair of shoes.

She was never afterwards quite sure as to when she had taken the final decision. Perhaps the moon itself tempted her to make the rash attempt. Though obligingly rising at a time convenient to her purpose, it was just past the full, and the knowledge that she would have to wait another month before conditions were again so propitious was not to be endured.

And then, on the next two nights when she might have made the attempt, there were lights in the adjacent room indicating occupation. Having screwed her courage to sticking point it was maddening to be frustrated. She spent the whole of the third day on the balcony trying to decide whether the room was still being used, and was so moody and distrait that poor Ameera told Phoebe that she greatly feared that the missy was contemplating the shocking crime of self destruction. She had done nothing all day but lean on the balustrade and stare into space.

To Phoebe this was the last straw. A fortnight had passed since Russet had been brought to Furze House. Mr James had expected an easy victory over one whom he had described as a spoiled, petted chit. It seemed to Phoebe that her own reading of Miss Ingram's character was far nearer the truth and that the situation was now completely out of hand. She demanded an interview with the master, determined to tell him that if she was not permitted to see the prisoner and judge for herself, she would be obliged to leave his service. It would be like tearing the heart out of her body to do it, for he was as dear to her as her own child, but she could not stand by and see murder done. And if Ameera was right this was worse than murder–to be driving a helpless girl to encompass her own death.

Mr Cameron was out, said Ahmed Khan, but planned to be back by dinner time. The butler, too, had his anxieties. His precious daughter was grieving sadly over this awkward business and he did not want her to be involved in any trouble over her innocent share in it.

England was a strange country. His master's behaviour, never before questioned, was odd to say the least of it. He suggested that after dinner would be a good time for Phoebe to deliver her ultimatum.

Russet kept watch over her projected escape route throughout the afternoon. The windows remained closed until evening. Then, by leaning over her balcony, she could distinctly see the slim brown hands that pushed up the sashes. At which point she was obliged to desert her observation post because Ameera brought in her dinner tray.

She made only a pretence of eating. Her inner tension made swallowing difficult. Tonight, if only those inviting windows remained unlit, she was determined to make the attempt. As soon as Ameera had removed her tray would be the best time. The other occupants of the house would still be at table for if the meals served to her were any criterion they evidently appreciated good food. Gentlemen, too, were apt to linger over their wine. She could probably count on an hour at least before there was any likelihood of her escape being discovered. It was not very long but it would have to suffice. She had put on her plainest gown, so that there would be no frills or ruffles to catch on the brickwork. It would be the work of a moment to slip the well-filled purse in the bosom of her dress. There was a long walk ahead of her and she might have to hide from a determined pursuit but once free of the house she would make her way to freedom somehow. Carefully she refrained from contemplation of the ordeal that must be the prelude to escape, dwelling instead on the probable lay-out of the house and the chances of finding doors and gates conveniently open. At least, she comforted herself, it was a reasonably modern building. She was unlikely to lose herself in a labyrinth of mouldering passages.

And it seemed that at last everything was in her favour. The windows remained open and no light shone from them. The night was not quite so dark as she would have liked but she dared not wait for full dark to fall. Even the moon smiled upon her enterprise, casting a soft clear light on that frightening ledge. In fact it proved surprisingly easy to climb over the balustrade and take the first two or three steps along the ledge, her hands wide-spread, palms flattened against bricks that still retained the warmth of the sun, advancing one foot cautiously, then sliding the other up to it. Easy enough—for just so long as she could see the familiar balustrade out of the corner of her eye and know that by stretching out a hand she could draw herself back to safety. But alas! The illusion lasted for only half a dozen steps. Then she was fairly launched on the traverse. Small use to tell herself that the ledge was as safe as a sidewalk. She pressed herself against the wall so desperately that the fabric of her gown rubbed and caught against the roughness of the mortar, and the tiny jerks as it held fast or pulled free terrified her, threatening to shake her into the abyss. Her hands were clammy with perspiration, her whole body wet with it. There was a thundering in her ears, a choking in her throat. Her breath came quick and shallow, for even a deep breath might destroy her precarious balance. And she thought of nothing in the world but of advancing one foot and painstakingly bringing the other up to it.

She shut her eyes tightly lest involuntarily she should glance down and so she did not see the glow of light that sprang up in those beckoning windows, nor the rigid figure that watched her progress in a tension of fear that surpassed her own, since he could do nothing but wait. When at last her arm brushed against the balcony railing she could not immediately believe that she had made the crossing safely. Her hand fumbled blindly for the support of the iron. There was a sudden fierce grip on her wrist that left blue bruises for a week, and a strong arm scooped her up by the waist and lifted her bodily over the railing.

For a moment, in her passion of relief, she did not realise that the great effort had been in vain. She clung to the smooth iron, her head bowed against it, retching uncontrollably as waves of nausea swept over her, beyond coherent speech, beyond any further physical effort. Then savage fingers bit into her shoulders, drawing her upright, thrusting her towards the open window.

"Reckless irresponsible little fool!" he shot at her, venting the fury aroused by his own great fear on its innocent cause. "Are you quite mad? Is it not enough that you have wrecked Letty's happiness and set my whole household by the ears with your pathetic attitudes? Must you hurl yourself to destruction from my very windows? I suppose you see yourself as a figure of high tragedy and picture us all mourning remorsefully over your pitiful broken body. And all to be laid at *my* door because I ventured to put a stop to your mischievous tricks."

The girl between his hands looked up at him wanly. The knowledge of failure was bitter, now, within her, and she was still sick and giddy. She said slowly, "It very nearly was, wasn't it?" And then, seeing his look of puzzlement, added fretfully, weakly, "My broken body laid at your door," and slipped from his hold to the floor in a crumpled heap.

She was back in her own room when she opened her eyes again, and it was Phoebe who was hanging anxiously over her and who broke into affectionate scolding when she essayed a feeble smile.

"Now that's better, Miss Russet. What a naughty girl you are, to be sure, giving us all such a fright. Here. Just you drink this. Nasty stuff it is, I know, but the master says it's what you need, with you so sick-like."

Russet surveyed the golden liquid in the beautiful glass with dreamy interest—and smiled at her attendant, a smile of such confiding warmth that Phoebe was quite startled.

"And when I have swallowed it, I shall feel very much more the thing," she quoted reminiscently.

"Well I wouldn't know about that, miss," replied Phoebe practically. "More likely to put you to sleep *I* should say. But no harm in that after what you've gone through tonight. And since the master says you must drink it, down it must go."

Russet, recovering fast in this nursery atmosphere, raised a dissident eyebrow, but to please Phoebe she consented to sip a little of what proved to be brandy. She endorsed Phoebe's verdict that it was nasty stuff but could not deny that it banished the nausea and made her brain feel surprisingly clear and determined. Sipping slowly, she eventually finished the dose, which Mr Cameron had poured with a generous hand.

"Is—HE—very angry?" she demanded valiantly. "Because he has only himself to blame. I hope he has not scolded you or Ameera, because my escape—near escape," she corrected ruefully, "was no fault of yours."

Phoebe chuckled. "In all the years I've known him I disremember ever seeing him so put about. Did he rail at you? 'Twould be because you'd given him such a fright. He was near as white as you were when he rang for me, and the bell pealing fit to bust your ear-drums. Which didn't surprise me when he told me what you'd done," she added in final admonition. "But all's well that ends well and you've come to no lasting harm."

"And am still a prisoner," put in Russet quietly.

Phoebe looked uncomfortable. "Yes, miss. And I had to give him my solemn promise that I wouldn't help you to escape before he'd let me stay with you."

Russet smiled at her. "I won't try to tempt you from your allegiance," she said, "nor keep you any longer from your sleep, even though it *is* so very comfortable to have you about me again. Ameera is a dear little soul but naturally it is not the same."

"Well as to that, miss," muttered poor Phoebe awkwardly, "the master said as I'm to stop with you all night, 'case you was to try any more foolhardy tricks," she explained shamefaced.

Russet stared at her in outrage. "I wonder

that he does not have me fettered and chained," she exclaimed. "Monstrous!"

From the expression on Phoebe's face it was plain that there was more to follow. "He did speak of having the windows barred, for safety's sake," she confessed reluctantly. "But maybe by tomorrow, when he's had time to get over his fright, he'll think better of it."

"I should certainly hope so! To be treating me as though I were an infant or an imbecile! He would be well served it I *did* make another attempt to break free. But I couldn't do it, Phoebe. Not even if I were to stun you with the poker and tie you up with the bedclothes. Which, you will agree, would only give you your just deserts after the way you served *me*."

There was laughter in the urchin grimace that accompanied this dire threat but it died swiftly as she went on, "I wouldn't face that crossing again even if Mr Cameron himself said that I might go free if I accomplished it. I shall just have to stay here until that wretched young pair settle their differences."

"Well as to that, miss," volunteered Phoebe eagerly, "Mr Cameron was visiting at Dene Court today—that's where Mrs Waydene lives. Maybe he's heard how matters are going on, though of course he wouldn't confide in the likes of me. And being shut up won't be so bad, will it now, with Phoebe to keep you company and tell you all that's going on in the house?"

"It will if I have to submit to having bars across the window," objected Russet firmly, "and so you may tell the head jailer. But it will be the greatest comfort to me to have your society," she relented. And then, with a twinkle, "I daresay I shall find you more conversible than Chimi!"

It was Phoebe's turn to snort her indignation. "Too much brandy, Miss Russet, that's what's the matter with you! And enough of your funning. Time you was asleep."

"And you?"

"I shall do very nicely on the day-bed, here. And you'll be a good girl and not get up to any more mischievous larks, won't you, now?"

As a description of her ordeal it was the understatement of all time. It made Russet chuckle. It even dispelled some of the lingering horror of that ordeal. She agreed that she was indeed tired and that no doubt things would look better in the morning, and bade her attendant an affectionate good night.

Chapter Seven

The master of Furze House had slept badly after the shattering experience of his prisoner's attempted escape, and woke in an unsettled state of mind. On the previous day he had driven out to Dene Court, thankful to bid farewell for a while to the growing gallery of reproachful faces that surrounded him, and hoping that the tedious duty visit that he proposed to pay might offer some prospect of an early end to his present discomforts. It was really quite absurd that one insignificant girl, locked up in circumstances of more than adequate comfort, should have such a disruptive effect on his household. Why! A strict guardian might keep a rebellious ward on bread and water for a week; might even beat her to enforce submission, and no one would say a word against him. It was true that Miss Ingram was *not* his ward. But Letty was. And surely he had a right to safeguard her interests in the only way that was open to him? *Was* it necessary for Phoebe and Ameera to look at him as though he was little better than the public hangman? Even Herrick, closely questioned, had stoutly declared that Miss Ingram had seemed to him a very pleasant and sensible young lady, and one that was considerate of her servants.

If he found relief in leaving this atmosphere of general disapproval behind, he was less fortunate in the other aspect of his visit. Both Mrs and Miss Waydene were at home, but the elder lady greeted him with unaccustomed reserve and the younger was downright peevish. It was the first time that Mr Cameron had seen the unpleasant side of his ward and it came as a distinct shock. So far as Letty was concerned, the world was out of tune and she did not care who knew it. She had set her heart on ending her first season with the triumphant announcement of her betrothal and forthcoming marriage. Now, partly because of Russet Ingram but chiefly because Lucian had been careless and clumsy, it was all spoiled. It might be true, as Lucian claimed, that he had gone down to Southampton to inspect a yacht that he thought of buying and not, after all, to bid a fond farewell to Miss Ingram. But surely he was old enough to look where he was going and to avoid ridiculous mishaps that upset Miss Letty's plans? To her guardian's civil enquiries about Staneborough's progress she returned sullen answers. She had not seen him—could not be forever writing letters—supposed his bones would mend in time. Her mama frowned, but indulgently, upon this rather heartless and unbecoming attitude, but expressed the view that Lucian must show himself more careful and sensible before she would feel inclined to entrust her darling to his keeping. A change of front indeed, thought Mr Cameron, and politely suggested that if the ladies wished to visit the invalid he would be very happy to drive them to Southampton where young Staneborough was still recuperating at the home of his yacht-owning friend. The offer was declined with a promptitude that aroused all his suspicions, and these were considerably strengthened by the arrival of another visitor. He knew Robert Dysart perfectly well by sight—the lad had been for ever dancing attendance on Letty—but in face of his ward's avowal of her love for Staneborough, Mr Cameron had paid him small heed. It seemed to him now that the young man was very much at home; was greeted with marked distinction by the older lady, and with shy welcome, hastily assumed, by the younger. With disillusioned eyes Mr Cameron saw much that had escaped him before. The roguish smiles, the sparkling vivacity with which his ward was beglamouring her new admirer were in such marked contrast to the demeanour that she had shown *him* that he could not help recognising their artificiality. He declined Mrs Waydene's offer of refreshment and was not pressed to stay. Letty, restored to good humour by Robert Dysart's visit, gave him her sunniest smile at parting. She bore small resemblance to the doleful little creature who had proclaimed her love for Staneborough and had begged his help. Mr Cameron decided that he would never understand the workings of the female mind.

It was a very thoughtful gentleman who drove back to Furze House. He was a proud man, accustomed to wielding absolute authority; not one who would easily confess to error. But he was also a man of integrity, and the more he considered the evidence the more he was reluctantly compelled to admit that he might have done Miss Ingram a grave injustice. A little late in the day he recalled those slight inconsistencies which had puzzled him at the time and which he had dismissed as trivial. He came to the conclusion that a carefully casual call on Staneborough might be a useful exercise. Their acquaintance was of the slightest but he could make the excuse that he had thought the invalid might like news of Letty while he was laid by the heels. He was not yet prepared to exonerate Miss Ingram completely but it might be helpful to enquire a little further into her relations with Letty's future husband. If, indeed, on this afternoon's showing, Staneborough still stood in that position.

In his preoccupation he actually allowed the bays to dawdle, and as a consequence was late home. Since he was thoughtful of his servants and was, in any case, dining alone, he decided not to delay matters further by changing his dress and sat down to dinner in his riding clothes. Russet had been far out in her calculations here. Mr Cameron certainly appreciated good food but ate sparingly, and he had never been one for sitting over his wine. Which was fortunate on this occasion since he was called upon to endure a most uncomfortable interview with his housekeeper.

Phoebe was too damned convincing. His conscience, already restive where his dealings with Miss Ingram were concerned, began to rebel in earnest. Moreover it was manifestly unfair to leave the responsibility for his captive's welfare to the servants if she was behaving in so peculiar a fashion. He would have to see the girl for himself and the sooner the better. But since his code of courtesy would not permit him to visit a lady—even a prisoner—in riding dress, first he must change into more formal garb. It was with this object in view that he had gone up to his room, there to be drawn to the open window by sounds indicative of an attempt at stealthy entrance and to discover Miss Ingram in the middle of her perilous passage.

He devoutly hoped that he would never again be required to live through another such aeon of paralysed helplessness. The moonlight had spared him nothing; the tightly closed eyes; the under lip, caught so fiercely between white teeth that a tiny bead of blood showed black on the fair skin; the desperate clutching fingers. And himself a useless frozen image, because the least sound or movement might break the tension of determination that held her and he would have to watch her hurtle helplessly to her death.

Small wonder that he had unleashed the full fury of his rage over her, once he had her safe. And she, sick and shaken as she was, had come back at him with a jest. Some foolish quip in response to his remark about her fate being laid at his door. Not very subtle, perhaps. But the sheer courage of the girl! And then she had collapsed and he had summoned Phoebe. Mr Cameron, who listed courage and truthfulness about equal at the head of the moral qualities that he respected, found himself compelled to unwilling admiration. Miss Ingram's truthfulness might still be open to question but there could be no doubting her courage.

He was down betimes next morning making his usual round of the stables, but so absent was his manner that even the head groom decided to leave him severely alone instead of launching into the detailed report and commentary in which he was used to indulge. He lingered over his breakfast, too, though he would have been hard put to it to say what he had eaten, and poured himself a second cup of coffee before he decided to summon Ameera.

The girl seemed frightened, but he spoke to her in her own tongue so kindly and gently that Miss Ingram would scarcely have recognised him, and it was not long before she was telling him of her pity for the prisoner's loneliness and of her idea of introducing Chimi by way of entertainment and company. Since they had aired the topic pretty thoroughly in the kitchen quarters, she even confessed to the belief that it was Chimi's acrobatic prowess that had given Miss Ingram the idea of attempting the ledge. But how could she have dreamed of such a thing, pleaded poor Ameera. And had to be consoled and assured that no one thought her in the least to blame.

He dismissed her presently, asking her to send Phoebe to him and straitly enjoining her not to leave Miss Ingram until Phoebe returned. Not that he really imagined the girl would try to repeat last night's exploit, but he was taking no risks.

A long conference with Phoebe left him in something of a quandary. As that good soul had foretold he had thought better of his threat to have the windows barred, but he was not yet ready to agree to the prisoner's unconditional release. He was fast coming round to the opinion that either he had totally misread the situation or—grimly—that he had been deliberately misled. But he had gone to some trouble to arrange the abduction of Miss Ingram and until he was wholly convinced, he preferred to keep her under his hand. The problem was how to achieve this and, at the same time, guard against such dangerous tricks as she had essayed last night.

A suggestion from Phoebe that Miss Russet should be asked to pledge her word to make no further attempt at escape met with a shake of the head and an amused lift of a disbelieving eyebrow. That aroused her indignation. "A decent woman has just as good a notion of honour and faithfulness to her pledged word as any man," she told him roundly. "Maybe more, because she has good sense as well. You'd not find a woman leaving her tradesfolk's bills unpaid while she strained every nerve and impoverished her own family to pay some ridiculous gaming debt."

"As Miss Ingram's father did," pointed out her employer.

"Well—there you are then," retorted Phoebe, with incontrovertible feminine logic. "She *is* an Ingram. Surely you can take her word?"

Mr Cameron was not convinced. He decided

to discuss the matter with his prisoner. But the reports of his two underlings gave him much food for thought and presently sent him once more to the stables. His unexpected appearance caused some surprise but no alarm. He was too strict a master for there to be any likelihood of slackness. In fact he exchanged a few pleasant comments with his head groom, received a satisfactory report on the progress of the black colt destined for a racing career, and wended his way towards the humbler servitor who was charged principally with the welfare of his dogs. After a brief but highly technical conference with this worthy he accepted delivery of a small wriggling bundle which he tucked under one arm, since it was just too large to go into the capacious pocket of his driving coat, and returned to the house.

Though this was not precisely his intent, the pup certainly served to remove any constraint that he might have felt over his interview with Miss Ingram. Set down on four widely splayed legs she skated perilously on the polished oak boards, wiggled an ecstatic rump at her hostess and promptly squatted to make a puddle. By the time that Mr Cameron had snatched her up again and dumped her outside on the verandah and Phoebe, scolding vigorously, had mopped up the evidence, Miss Ingram's pale little face had relaxed into something approaching its usual friendly air.

"Which you should have known what she'd do, sir, and her not two months old and motherless at that, poor little soul," ended Phoebe. "If you're thinking to leave her with Miss Russet she'll need a tray of soil. *And* a basket to sleep in, or we'll have her making free with the chairs which is what I don't hold with. I'll go and see Heaton about it right away."

"Should you like to keep the little thing?" enquired Mr Cameron rather stiffly as the door closed behind her. "I'm afraid she'll make a good deal of work and need constant watching, but it might be an interest for you, and Phoebe tells me you are in need of something of the kind. Do you care for dogs?"

Miss Ingram said that she did. "Though I have never before had dealings with one so young," she added thoughtfully. And then, watching the pup, who had already forgotten her lapse from grace and was investigating the balcony furnishings with lively curiosity, "What is she? She has something of the look of my cousin's pug, but surely she is too big?"

"Much too big—and of a very different temperament. She's a bull bitch, the only survivor of the litter. Her dam died in whelping and Heaton has brought her up by hand so she is friendly and trustful. Full grown she'll be a first-rate guard for her owners and their property," he told her, thankful to be able to converse on an impersonal topic.

It seemed that Miss Ingram also subscribed to this idea. "But are they not the dogs that are used in baiting bears and bulls?" she enquired. "And sometimes, I believe, in fighting other dogs, so that men may bet on the result."

Her jailer looked grim. "That is so," he admitted. "Though I trust that you are not adding the notion of my breeding dogs for such purposes to the rest of the crimes that you hold against me. The bulldog's courage is universally acknowledged. But because he looks slow and easy-going, gamesters will often put their money on some more active, savage-seeming dog—usually to the financial profit of the bulldog owner. For my part I abhor all such practices."

He stopped abruptly. He had been on the verge of explaining how he had bought the pitiful bitch, heavily in whelp, from a brutal master; how he and Heaton had sat up all night with her when the pups were born; had used all their skill and patience in the vain attempt to save her. But it was no part of his scheme to appeal to Miss Ingram's sympathies. He began to understand, in some small measure, the quality in her that drew her legions of admirers. She was a listener; not just waiting to air her own views, but truly interested in what you were saying. Even in the present unpropitious circumstances her small pale wedge of a face lit with animation as she listened to his remarks about the pup and her breed. But he refused to be so easily seduced, however innocent the topic. There was renewed stiffness in his voice as he said, "If you wish to keep the pup, she will need exercise. Phoebe assures me that I may safely trust to the honour of an Ingram. If you will give me your promise that you will not try to escape, you may walk in the gardens each day."

She took a moment or two to think this over. Then she said slowly, "I will not promise not to make a bid for freedom if opportunity offers. But if you will trust me with the puppy I will not use her as a pretext. While I am walking her in the garden you may rely on my promise."

He considered her thoughtfully. It was a reasonable compromise—and more convincing, he felt, than more fulsome avowals.

"Will you also promise me that you will not again risk your life by attempting *that* way of escape?" He jerked his head towards the open window.

There was no pretence about the nervous little shiver, hastily controlled, or the convulsive clenching of her hands. But her voice was quiet and unemotional as she said, "That I will promise without reserve."

"Then you will ring for Ameera when you wish to go out," he instructed.

She nodded. And, on an afterthought, asked impulsively, "What is her name? The puppy."

"As yet she has none. You may choose for her. Only"—for the first time she saw his rueful, twisted grin—"nothing too fanciful, I beg of you. Remember how she will look when she is grown!"

With that he left her, absorbed and amused as she had not been since she had been snatched out of her ordered comfortable life.

The pattern of her days changed rapidly. The pup was young and needed frequent walking. There were her meals to be supervised—she was a greedy eater and apt to choke—and romping games to be devised or she grew bored and destructive. She was also firmly convinced that she was a lap-dog and clambered confidently into Russet's lap whenever she felt the need of a brief nap to restore her energies. She was, in fact, a full time occupation and a very rewarding one, being both intelligent and affectionate.

Their first excursions were rather stilted affairs, Russet feeling awkward at the formality of being escorted to the terrace by no less a person than Ahmed Khan himself, grave-faced and imposing in his morning livery of snowy white linen and intricately twisted turban, the puppy excited and alarmed by her introduction to the restriction of collar and leash. And that makes two of us, thought Russet wryly, for she too felt that she had been let out to a very limited freedom. The grounds at Furze House were not large. No more than eight or nine acres had been laid out as park—or, more accurately, as 'wild' garden, since it had been skillfully planted with shrubs and furnished with winding grassy paths that made the most of its limited size. All the rest was formal garden, terraces, flower beds and lawns, the latter of such velvety smoothness that one could not even contemplate permitting a puppy to sully their perfection.

Russet felt that the wild garden was the most suitable for her charge's needs, but the pup, as she had already discovered, had a will of her own. Having accepted the discipline of the leash and indulged her mistress with a full investigation of her kingdom, she decided that she preferred people and activities to rustic solitude. Since Russet had no particular objection to following where she was led, it was amazing how often their walks ended at the stables—where his fosterling was always sure of a warm welcome from Heaton—or in the kitchen premises, which a keen nose had early learned to associate with food. Before the week was out the pair of them were a familiar sight in every corner of the grounds. Herrick had greeted Miss Ingram with delight and insisted on showing her round the stables, where she petted satiny muzzles and was permitted to feed one or two old pensioners with favourite titbits. She might have been an honoured guest. Only when she returned to her own room did she recall that she was still a prisoner, and even then the recollection was no longer oppressive, since she had but to ring for Ameera or Phoebe if she wished to go out again.

Since she was of a friendly and forthright disposition and since all the servants treated her with respect, her walks abroad began to assume the nature of a royal progress. Ahmed Khan would bow her out. There would be gardeners eager to draw her attention to some choice bloom that had opened overnight, or a stable boy looking expectantly for a friendly smile or a word of greeting. Phoebe would come bustling out to ask if she would not like a glass of cool lemonade after her exertions, and Herrick openly regretted that the master's orders prevented him from driving her out to see some of the pretty countryside so much admired by visitors.

Mr Cameron, who had been called to Town on urgent business before he had been able to pay his intended call on Staneborough, was sadly shaken on his return to discover the change that had taken place in his household during his ten days' absence.

He rode in on a scene of innocent merriment. The bull pup, in an unguarded moment, had made off with a surcingle, and, with small teeth set firmly in the leather, was refusing to surrender it, despite command and blandishment. Russet, perched on a mounting block, was chuckling triumphantly over the failure of Heaton to win obedience where she herself had already lamentably failed. Herrick and two of the stable staff were offering advice, helpful or humorous. So much met Mr Cameron's amazed and affronted gaze at first glance. His incisive, "Drop it!" was more effective than an incantation. One groom promptly melted away into the comforting gloom of the stable while the other sprang forward to take his horse. Heaton surrendered the end of the strap that he was holding to Herrick, called the two pointers to heel and departed with unusual celerity, and the pup actually *did* drop the strap, though more from eagerness to greet the newcomer than from any notion of obedience. Only Miss Ingram and Herrick remained outwardly unmoved, Herrick because he was legitimately concerned with the fate of the purloined surcingle, Russet because she refused to show any sign of apprehension in the presence of the enemy. For all his keen assessing glance, he could not know how fast her heart was beating at this unexpected confrontation.

The arrival of Phoebe, buxom and beaming, bearing a tray that held a glass of milk and a plate of rout cakes, offered final proof—if any were needed—of the quiet revolution that had been taking place at Furze House during his absence. So trivial a task would normally have been delegated to the newest and youngest maidservant. That Phoebe should assume it indicated that the mantle of her approval and protection had now been cast firmly over his prisoner. He caught something about—"so thin as you are, I thought milk might set you up better than lemonade," and had a ridiculous impulse to protest that the thinness was none of his doing; that the girl had birdbones, had been no more than a slip of a thing when first he had seen her. He managed to restrain it and said with solemn politeness that he trusted that Miss Ingram was enjoying good health. With matching gravity the lady informed him that her health was always excellent and, for good measure, enquired if he had had a comfortable journey.

This sparkling exchange apparently exhausted their conversational resources, and since Phoebe, having curtsied her greetings to her master, was engaged in furnishing Herrick with a long list of stores that she wanted the undergroom to purchase for her, there was an awkward little hiatus. Fortunately the pup did not appreciate the tension of the situation. She had become accustomed to being the centre of attention and when an imperative, "Yip!" failed to recall her humans to their duties, she proceeded to remedy matters by launching a growling attack on Mr Cameron's riding boots. His explosive, "No!" and Russet's, "Stop it, Jai!" came together, and so abashed the culprit that she rolled over on her back and, with all four paws waving helplessly in the air, endeavoured to explain that it was a complete misunderstanding. She had intended merely to *polish* the gleaming leather by the assiduous application of a small pink tongue. They had to laugh. Whereupon a pair of big dark eyes gleamed mischievously at them and the pup raced off after a leaf that was drifting in the gentle breeze.

"*What* did you call her?" asked Mr Cameron, still smiling. "Jay? Well—at least it has the merit of being short." He studied the pup, now rolling rapturously in the sunshine which showed the golden beige of her coat, barred and dappled with black, in all its gleaming beauty. "I suppose it was her colouring that gave you the notion," he conceded dubiously, "but I trust she will not prove so noisy as her namesake."

"Not Jay! Jai," she corrected, giving the initial 'J' its soft French pronunciation. And as he still looked puzzled, "Because she will never let go. What I have, I hold, might well serve as her motto, so J'ai seemed a good name for her."

"You speak French?"

She laughed. "Because I know the first person singular of the verb avoir? Schoolgirl French, only, and spoken with a very English accent, I am told."

"My mother preferred it to English," he explained, "so to me it is the language of childhood. Very apt—your name. I like it. And has Jai proved a satisfactory companion for you?"

"So much so that I hope you mean to sell her to me when I go. I should be loath indeed to lose her now."

He smiled, but shook his head slightly. "She is not really a lady's dog, you know. Not smart or fashionable. You could not tuck her into your muff even now, and she is growing apace. Nor do I think she would really care for the social round. But we need not concern ourselves with that question at the moment."

Russet, however, refused to be hinted away. She said resolutely, "It is close on a month that you have held me here. The time when you could count on doing so without awkward questions being asked is running out. When do you propose to let me go?"

His expression hardened perceptibly, but his voice was still pitched in a pleasantly conversational tone as he said, "That I cannot say at this present. Perhaps I shall be able to give you more precise information at the end of the week. In the meanwhile I will do what is possible to make your captivity less irksome. Though from what I can see"—his face was transformed by that characteristic grin—"you already enjoy the status of honoured guest. Quite one of the family, in fact."

She said defensively, "I have kept my promise. It is true that I have had a great deal of liberty, but it was for Jai's sake, and I have not abused it. I have not even attempted to spy out the land—to discover in what direction the nearest village lies, for instance, and *that*, you know, I might very well have done without breaking the actual letter of my promise."

"You are a very unusual female, ma'am," he told her. And now there was laughter mellowing the timbre of the deep voice. "So much so that I will venture another suggestion. Give me your—your parole d'honneur, and I will permit you to drive out—or to ride if you prefer it—for a little while each day. You must be heartily sick of this restricted scene."

She hesitated. The offer was tempting—he was perfectly right about the monotony of the garden, delightful as it was—but acceptance would still further limit the time in which she could legitimately attempt escape.

He said thoughtfully, "I could not permit you to go into the village, of course. Not that I imagine you would use such a visit to further an attempt at freedom. It is just that, in your own interest, it would be better for your presence in my home to remain a secret."

"It is rather late in the day for you to be considering my reputation," suggested Russet tartly. "For I must suppose that that is what you mean. Very well, sir. I will accept your kindly suggestion, but only because I believe that you will very shortly be obliged to let me go without any particular effort on my part."

"That we shall see," he returned pleasantly. "As I informed you at the outset, you will be free to go as soon as my ward has settled her affairs, which must, I think, be very soon."

"You are certainly a very conscientious guardian," she said drily. "When I consider what I have been called upon to endure merely because you *imagined* that I had come between Letty and Staneborough, I must confess that I would not lightly choose to cross your will."

"Then you will oblige me by taking Herrick with you if you wish to drive," he retorted promptly. "Either the phaeton or the whiskey, whichever you prefer, and I have no objection to you driving yourself so long as you have someone reliable with you. If you prefer to ride, perhaps you would permit *me* to accompany you–at least until I can be sure that my horses are not too strong for you."

"Your concern for my well-being is most commendable, sir. Or is it, perhaps, concern for your horses?"

He looked her straight in the eyes. "You deal shrewd blows, Miss Ingram. I am well aware that I deserved that one. I can only plead that you stood in little real danger from the 'accident' that delivered you into my hands. The place had been most carefully chosen, the timing well rehearsed. And may I further suggest that if my concern was only for my horses I might well hesitate before entrusting them to so daring and reckless a lady as you have shown yourself."

For a moment the issue hung in the balance. But Russet's longing for a wider liberty and a certain justice in his remarks eventually won the day.

"Shall we agree that honours are evenly divided?" she suggested, with a lurking twinkle. And added, as the grave countenance relaxed to an answering smile, "I shall be happy to accept of your escort. No doubt you will be tired today, after your journey. But if you should feel inclined to ride with me tomorrow I will be grateful."

Chapter Eight

That first ride had been arranged for the early morning, since they were agreed that the cool of the day was better for the horses and pleasanter for the riders. It had been rather longer than the usual hour's exercise. Once he had taken stock of Miss Ingram's equestrian capabilities there had seemed to be a great deal to talk about. Beginning impersonally enough with the beauty of the countryside and the vagaries of an English summer, they had moved swiftly to an animated discussion on horses, the different methods of breaking and training them and the suitability of hunting as a sport for females. But the horses grew restive, unaccustomed to such lazy loitering, and had to be let out to shake the fidgets out of them. Mr Cameron was granted an excellent opportunity of noting that, though Miss Ingram might not care for the notion of females in the hunting field, it was not from lack of pluck—though that, of course, he already knew—nor from incompetence. Though she made no parade of her skill she might have been born in the saddle. The mare that he had, with some misgivings, selected for her use, was a rare handful. No vice, of course, but full of spirit and playful tricks. Naturally there were no animals in his stable that could truthfully be described as ladies' mounts, which was why he had insisted that he himself should escort Miss Ingram if she wished to ride. It had been plain from the outset that the lady was no novice. The sympathy between rider and mount had been allowed to develop naturally. The slender hands were firm and capable. Mr Cameron, watchful and alert as the horses broke into a canter, saw the little smile of content as Miss Ingram gave herself to enjoyment of the rhythm and presently suggested that the stretch of smooth turf at the top of the down would be ideal for a short gallop. She nodded briefly and touched the mare with her heel.

By the time that the pair trotted sedately back into the stable yard, Mr Cameron had stopped concerning himself with his companion's safety and, save for such courtesies as opening and closing gates, left her to manage for herself. When he held up his hands to help her dismount she accepted the attention unselfconsciously and thanked him with patent sincerity for the pleasure of the ride. It seemed perfectly natural to suggest that she should breakfast with him, and if her slight hesitation reminded him briefly of their respective rôles as prisoner and jailer it was soon over. She accepted without comment, since she felt it would be ungracious to refuse when he had exerted himself to be kind. Besides—she wanted to accept. Breakfast with Mr Cameron promised more entertainment than her usual solitary repast.

But the morning ride had now become a daily occurrence which neither of them would have dreamed of missing. Indeed, each day as they returned they would plan where they would go tomorrow. And somehow it seemed to be more convenient for Mr Cameron to share the pleasure of tooling the phaeton about the lanes in the drowsy afternoon heat rather than for Herrick to neglect his other duties. Sharing breakfast after the morning ride seemed only sensible and it was really Phoebe who was responsible for initiating their practice of dining together. Their breakfast table conferences grew longer and longer until one day she came to enquire, with due deference, if they would mind removing to the drawing room or the library, as the maids were waiting to put the room to rights for luncheon.

They had been discussing agricultural practices in Scotland, in particular the 'run-rig' system, in which a number of tenants shared and worked a communal farm. Russet had never heard of it, and Mr Cameron had been condemning it with fluency and fervour, for the prosperity of the land of his forebears was very dear to him. He accepted Phoebe's interruption absently and suggested that they remove to the library where he could produce documents to show how desperately reform was needed, how rewarding were the results when a stubborn and tradition-ridden native populace could at last be persuaded to try modern methods.

"It doesn't help, of course, that originally they had to bring in English farmers to teach the new methods," he said teasingly, as he pulled out Russet's chair. "But the way things are going now, they'll soon be beating the Southrons at their own game."

He had opened the dining room door and stood aside for Russet to precede him when Phoebe spoke again. "You'll not be keeping Miss Russet over-long, will you, sir? There's that blessed pup yammering to go out and near driving poor Ameera crazy. Keeps running off with your slippers, miss, and as fast as Ameera gets one out of her jaws she makes off with another. Proper little madam she's getting to be."

Russet stopped, a dismayed hand going to her lips. In the interest of their talk she had forgotten all about the pup and it was long past the time for her morning walk. "If you will hold me excused, sir," she said guiltily, "I really ought to take Jai out. It is turned eleven."

Mr Cameron cast a startled glance at the hall clock. Phoebe said encouragingly, "Could you not let the Scottish farmers be until this evening? If you was to take dinner together you could sort them properly with none to hinder, but it's a shame to keep that pup indoors on so fine a day. All growing things need sunshine."

Since neither the lady nor the gentleman raised any objections to this proposal, that seemed to settle the matter, and Phoebe retired to her own domain, well pleased with her meddling in her employer's business. The affair was progressing very nicely, she decided. Mr James had not been so contented nor so cheerful since his mother's death. It was obvious—to Phoebe, at any rate—that a nice little wife was just what he needed. Maybe, after all, it had been a good day's work when she and Matthew had carried off Miss Russet.

They led an oddly isolated life at Furze House. It was natural enough, in view of their peculiar relationship, that Mr Cameron should choose the quiet tracks for their rides and make wide detours if they saw anyone about. When they were driving they did occasionally meet other vehicles but it seemed that he had few acquaintances in the neighbourhood for he never stopped to exchange greetings in the easy-going country fashion that could develop into a rambling discussion on local news until some other vehicle demanded the right of the road.

Once they drove along that narrow lane where Russet had met with an 'accident'. Mr Cameron did not remark on it, but she caught his swift sideways glance and, she thought, a hint of embarrassment in his bearing. She said impulsively, "Even in that horrid moment I had time to admire your command of your horses. But you will forgive me for saying that I prefer to be in the carriage *with* you!"

Though the remark was complimentary it was spoken with the blunt simplicity that a schoolboy might have used. Mr Cameron accepted it with a brief nod. But presently he said quietly, "Miss Ingram, your generosity puts me to shame. I shall never again use this particular lane without feeling a twinge of remorse for the risk I took."

"Well that is being foolish beyond permission," she said practically. "The lane is quite charming, if a trifle narrow. I took no hurt from being tipped into the ditch, except perhaps to my dignity, and am thoroughly enjoying my drive this afternoon. You might just as well decide, while you are indulging in this orgy of mortification, to pull down the balcony from my room. I'm sure I gave you quite as bad a fright as you gave me!"

He did not answer. She ventured a sideways peep, but he appeared to be concentrating on his horses—those same magnificent chestnuts—and his expression was unwontedly stern, even for him. Perhaps her frank remarks had reminded him, unpleasantly, that she was his prisoner and not his guest. She took refuge in a placid silence, having no patience with the theory that one must always maintain a flow of light, if meaningless, chatter. If she could have read his thoughts, she might have decided that it would be kinder to distract him, however frivolous the topic, for Mr Cameron was wrestling with devils.

One of them was an old acquaintance. How many times had he fallen into error through his overweening pride? But this time pride was fighting a losing battle. Mr Cameron was ready to admit that he had been wrong. The girl beside him was all that Phoebe had claimed and more. She was as direct and honest as the wide-eyed pup sitting between them. Letty might have misled him in all innocence, but she *had* misled him. This was not the kind of girl to filch another's lover. There was no greed in her, though there was a deal of warmth and zest for living. He remembered anew all that he had heard of her and in particular the innumerable conquests that were credited to her name—and wondered if any of those urgent suitors had ever kissed the soft red mouth.

For that was his second devil—a newcomer, this one, of untried strength. Later, perhaps, Mr Cameron might be grateful that his hands had been fully occupied with his horses; that it had been impossible to yield to the fierce, sweet temptation to gather Miss Ingram in his arms and seek forgiveness for his follies and a promise of future happiness. At the moment he felt only an irrational anger with the farmer whose gig caused him to call upon all his skill and judgement as they met and passed in that narrow way. Fortunately he was able to justify Miss Ingram's expressed confidence in his ability, but he said abruptly, "That was careless of me. I should have remembered that it was market day. We had best turn off at the cross roads or we shall be meeting quite a few vehicles whose drivers know me."

A captive must have some form of mental stimulation. Prisoners in less comfortable circumstances had been known to tame rats; to write poems on their dungeon walls, or even to carve grotesque heads on the crude furniture of their cells. Miss Ingram's fancy had lighted on the notion of making her jailer laugh—or at least smile—as often as possible. She even played a little game with herself, counting up the day's score each evening, pondering long over the vexed question of whether a half-smothered chuckle could justifiably be reckoned as a laugh, because a laugh counted two points and a smile only one.

It was doubtless in pursuit of this innocent form of entertainment that she now said demurely, "I make you my apologies, sir. I am sorry that my appearance should put you to the blush. May I plead, in extenuation, that it is some time since I have had the opportunity of going shopping. Do I really appear such an antidote that you are ashamed to be seen in my company? Perhaps in future it would be better for me to stay at home if you are likely to meet any of your friends."

This hopeful sally quite failed of its intent. Not a muscle moved in the grave countenance as he checked the horses and turned to survey her with every appearance of careful assessment. She was wearing a severely plain carriage dress of honey-gold sarsenet, quite devoid of trimming but beautifully draped about the shoulders to expose the slender column of her throat. Her hair was swept back from her face and allowed to fall in one gleaming curl on the left shoulder. A wide-brimmed shallow-crowned hat of fine Italian straw exactly matched the dress in colour. It was trimmed with narrow brown ribbon that fastened under her chin in a neat flat bow. Displayed in a shop window the entire toilet would have passed almost unnoticed, save by a very discerning eye. As Miss Ingram wore it, it was so exactly right that one was inclined to wonder why no other woman had made so happy a choice.

"When you were a small girl, Russet, did your Papa ever spank you for impudence?" asked Mr Cameron levelly.

Russet was so startled that she actually jumped. It was the first time that he had forgotten the formality of 'Miss Ingram' and he did not seem to have noticed his slip. She twinkled at him naughtily and said, "Oh no, sir. I had the happiest of childhoods. I daresay I was shockingly indulged. Certainly I cannot remember being punished and only rarely being scolded."

He nodded thoughtfully. "Yes. It shows, you know."

"That I was odiously spoiled?"

"Let us rather say that you were accustomed to being loved."

For some reason that made her blush. She hastened to give the subject a new turn, hoping that her shady hat would conceal the hot colour that she could feel suffusing her cheeks. "And you, sir? Were you, also, indulged and petted?"

He smiled for that. "If there is any kindness in me, I learned it from my mother," he said quietly. "In childhood I saw very little of my father who was busily engaged in laying the foundations of his fortune in India. I was sixteen when my mother and I went out to join him–my character already formed. My father, moreover, was already subject to the recurrent fever that was eventually to prove fatal, and was much concerned with teaching me all that I needed to know about his many business concerns so that I should be capable of dealing with my inheritance when failing health made it impossible for him to do so. I was very raw and ignorant and he was infinitely patient and kind, praising my efforts more, perhaps, than they merited. But he was a sick man and a disappointed one, and I, in any case, was long past the age for indulgence and petting. I admired and respected him, but I cannot pretend that I held him in the same degree of affection that I bestowed upon Mama."

During their long talks in the growing intimacy of this past week, Russet had learned a good deal about Mr Cameron. She understood, even if she did not always agree with, his views on a number of different topics, social, agricultural and political. But this was the first time that she had met him in reminiscent and confidential mood about his personal affairs. It behoved her to tread very softly, she felt, if she wished to learn more–as she did.

"A disappointed man?" she queried thoughtfully. "I think you do yourself an injustice. He must have been very proud of you. Have you not taken hold of the estate that he left you and caused it to flourish and multiply?"

It was the right note. "That, perhaps," he agreed indifferently. "I meant rather that he was disappointed in a deeper, more primitive desire. It was always his dream to make his fortune by his own endeavours—which, indeed, he did—and then to return to Scotland and settle there. If it was possible he meant to buy back the family home which had been escheated when *his* father was proscribed after '15. As things turned out he never set foot in Scotland. And perhaps in that he was fortunate, since I doubt he would have been deeply disappointed. The Scotland of my grandfather's memories died with the clans on Culloden moor."

"And your mother?" she probed gently.

"She understood his longing, since she, too, had been brought up in exile, though for her there was no hope of a return to the lands of her forefathers. But when my father died she was content to let his dream die with him and to make her home with me. When at last I was able to bring her to England, I could hardly expect her to support the Highland winters after so many years in India, and we found that this temperate Hampshire climate suited her pretty well. So I bought Furze House and established her here where I could visit her frequently and still attend to my business affairs in the city. She chose to live secluded, content with her garden and her books and her painting. She was too tired, she said, to start making new friends, and in fact she lived less than two years after we came here."

Russet had sometimes speculated about the lack of visitors at Furze House, especially since she had emerged from her own enforced seclusion. It was unusual, because country folk were given to a good deal of visiting, especially in the summer when the roads were good. Now she understood the virtual isolation in which Mr Cameron lived, and, being a friendly creature herself, shivered a little at the thought of his loneliness. Business acquaintances and a delicate if much loved mother. Such friends as he might have made in his youth were doubtless half a world away in India. And it did not sound as though there had been much time for youthful friendships. The father seemed to have been a stern taskmaster, a man obsessed by a dream and sparing no one, himself least of all, in its pursuit. Small wonder that the son, with such a background, should be reserved, arrogant and impatient of any who stood in his way. Like his father he would sweep aside all obstacles in pursuit of his chosen goal.

They sat long over dinner that night. Nor, this time, did Phoebe permit the maids to disturb them. They talked of many things. Russet learned that after much patient negotiation Mr Cameron was about to take possession of the home of his ancestors.

"And a sad state it is in," he told her ruefully, "with little more than the walls standing and they fire-blackened. While as for the land! It will take a fortune, and years of patient work to put it in good heart. But it is work worth doing; and the folk who till the farms are worth helping. Dour and obstinate, mistrusting anything new-fangled, but not afraid of hard work and loyal to the core, once that loyalty is won."

"And you will forsake the comforts of Furze House and Cavendish Square for a primitive existence in this Highland wilderness?"

"Thankfully," he nodded. He hesitated for a moment. He did not wish to appear critical of *her* way of life, yet for some inexplicable reason was anxious that she should understand his motives and approve his decision. At last he said slowly, "I am not accustomed to being idle, and Town life holds little appeal for me. If I had grown up in this country and gathered around me friends and acquaintances as one does in schooldays, it would probably be very different. As it is I feel an outsider, an onlooker, whenever I am obliged to attend some social function. I have learned to recognise a great many people and can exchange trivialities with them, but it goes no deeper than that. There is no time to develop a closer intimacy.

Under these circumstances I find parties boring. I shall keep on the Cavendish Square house because my business interests demand a London centre. I may sell this place—it was bought principally with my mother in mind. But that I have not finally decided. Certainly I shall expect to spend a great deal of each year in Scotland. The plans that I have in mind will require my constant personal supervision, not to say persuasion. Indeed"—he smiled a little—"if my name were not Cameron and my pedigree easily proven I doubt if I could even hope for success. It seems that in those parts it is still a name to conjure with. So much, at least, of my grandfather's Scotland survives."

Miss Ingram had much to occupy her mind when at last she retired to her room. She smiled a little as Ameera, having prepared her for bed, solemnly locked her in. No one had thought to tell the girl that this formality was now totally unnecessary. After all, Miss Ingram herself was the only person who was fully informed on this head, and it had struck her as tactically undesirable that her jailer should know that she no longer had the least desire to escape. Mr Cameron—James—she tried the name tentatively, for after all *he* had called her Russet—might be undecided about the state of his affections. Russet had no doubt at all about hers. She had been wooed by so many eligibles, some of them handsome, wealthy, titled, several of them extremely likeable, without so much as a quickened heart-beat. She had succumbed helplessly to just such a dour, single-minded, black-avised Scot as Mr Cameron had so feelingly described, who had abducted her and frightened her for no good reason but his own arrogant whim, and had then treated her with awkward kindness and opened his proud heart to her as, she judged, he had never done to any other woman than his mother. There was no understanding it at all, and Russet did not even try. She was too busy planning how she could coax him into offering for her. It would not be easy. He had made it abundantly clear that he had no thought of marriage. He was not the kind of man to invite a wife to share the hardships that he had described. Hardships that must obviously endure for some considerable time, despite the wealth at his disposal. He would scarcely have detailed the primitive conditions so fully if he had entertained any thought that she might see them for herself. Nevertheless her reflections were, on the whole, happy enough, and a tender little smile curved her mouth as she remembered his remarks about impudence. At least he was not wholly indifferent to her!

Mr Cameron's reflections were less pleasant. To have met, at last, the one girl whom he longed to win for his wife, and to have begun their acquaintance by serving her such a trick that she would never look at him! Even if he might have stood a chance with her at the beginning—and in his present mood of humility he could see little to recommend him to any woman—she could not be expected to forgive that abduction. And worse, in his own opinion, was the fact that he had refused to believe her. She had behaved with a royal generosity over the business of the contrived accident but that did not mean that she would be ready to entrust herself to his keeping. He brooded over the happiness that might have been his had he not permitted pride and ill temper to oust balanced judgement. In one respect Russet had done him less than justice. He would not have hesitated for a moment over asking her to share a future fraught with problems and discomforts. He paid her the compliment of believing that she would wish to share all his difficulties if—and it was a big "if"—she had given him her love.

He sighed abruptly, and picked up the two-day-old Gazette with the object of giving his thoughts a more practical direction. His eye fell on the date. He stared at it in indignant disbelief. It was not possible that more than a week had elapsed since his return from Town! He had meant to return within three or four days at most, for his negotiations had reached a stage of critical importance. If someone else stepped in and bought the place at this juncture it would be gone for good. Only a buyer who wanted it as badly as he did would be fool enough to pay an exorbitant price for a neglected estate and a tumble-down castle that was barely habitable. It was significant of his change of heart that he shrugged aside the possibility as negligible. Lingering in Hampshire as he had done might well have wrecked plans that he had cherished for years. Compared with the inevitability of losing Russet it did not seem to matter a great deal.

He had meant to go to Southampton to call on Staneborough, too. That visit was no longer necessary. Whatever the trouble between Letty and Staneborough he was ready to go bail that it was none of Russet's making. But he was seized by a sudden desire to see how Staneborough's attitude would strike him now that the scales had been removed from his eyes. He would pay that long delayed visit the very next day, he decided impulsively. He need not forego the morning ride. After breakfast would be time enough. And for once he would entrust Russet to Herrick if she wished to drive out in the afternoon.

He was well down the Southampton road next day before it occurred to him that if his interview with Staneborough proved to be as satisfactory as he confidently expected, he would have no further excuse for detaining Miss Ingram under his roof.

Chapter Nine

Left to her own devices, Russet decided to spend a lazy afternoon sunning herself on the terrace. The day was extremely hot, but she loved the heat and was blessed with one of those matt creamy skins that do not easily burn. After lunch she coaxed Jai to accompany her on a slow and strolling progress through the gardens, where an irate gardener complained that the pup had been raiding his raspberry canes.

"Just walks down the row and licks off all the ones she can reach," he elaborated, seeing Russet's air of disbelief.

Russet launched into a spirited defence of her pet, pointing out that she was a meat eater, rejecting even bread and milk, and vegetables, too, unless they were liberally soaked in meat broth, so that it was highly unlikely that she would take to a criminal career in fruit stealing. But the sight of a squat dark mask raised lovingly to a particularly fine raspberry that hung just out of reach, of a black nose quivering eagerly and sturdy forepaws bouncing up and down in an attempt to reach the tempting delicacy, caused her to change her plea. She smiled ruefully and apologetically at the gardener, picked the raspberry, which the pup promptly devoured with every appearance of enjoyment and the greed of one who had been starved for days, and promised that in future she would try to keep Jai out of the kitchen garden. The gardener unbent, said sadly that it would be a sore task—"made off with the pick of the strawberries, too"—and returned to his duties. Russet led her triumphant charge back to the terrace and bade her be seated. The pup, panting heavily, pink tongue lolling, collapsed at her feet.

There was plenty to occupy a girl's thoughts. Russet sat with a neglected novel on her lap and strove to keep from pondering the present whereabouts of James Cameron. He had said only that he was going to Southampton and would return as soon as possible. It was now three o'clock. How soon was 'as soon as possible'? She wondered what had taken him into Southampton but she knew that part of his business was concerned with shipping and cargoes of oriental produce and thought it probable that some such matter had demanded his personal attention.

She would have been both surprised and delighted if she could have been granted a sight of his present occupation. Mr Cameron had drawn a blank in his projected visit. Staneborough had been gone these three days past, explained his erstwhile host, and pressed hospitality on the visitor in the most friendly fashion, eager to tell him how well the invalid had mended—"a clean break, and will be as good as new in a pig's whisper"—and to describe the perfections of the yacht that he had sold to his friend and the glories of his own new purchase. "Bigger, d'ye see, and a better sea-boat. And me with Dolly and the boy to think about, we need more room. Must start the boy right, y'know—won't do to have him feeling sick as soon as she starts to pitch a bit."

It presently emerged that 'the boy' was two months old. Mr Cameron extricated himself at last, not sure whether to feel sorry for the child or envious of his happy host, who had obviously found a wife and a way of life that were his ideal of perfection. And better a sea-roving life than immurement in a derelict Scottish castle, he thought glumly. The discomforts could scarcely be worse and there would at least be constant variation of scene. He managed to evade offers of refreshment on the plea of business engagements and rode on to the Dolphin where he stabled his horse and ate an early luncheon. There was an hour to be whiled away before the noble animal could be considered sufficiently rested for the return, and he passed it, in highly unusual fashion, in sauntering among the shops, deciding what he would buy for Russet if only he was related to her in some degree that would permit the bestowal of gifts. It did not take him long to dispose, in imagination, of quite a considerable sum, because, apart from the goods on display, he was frequently reminded of something that would be essential to the comfort of—say—a wife, who was obliged to reside in a cool northern climate. Furs, obviously, would be a plain necessity, and he was solemnly debating the respective merits of sable and ermine when his eye fell upon a curious little object in the window of a shop that was mostly given over to a display of fine china. It looked rather lonely and out of place among the Bow and Worcester, a comical little china dog, some six inches long and no more than four or five in height. It was not really like the puppy, Jai, for it had a plumy tail and a heavy ruff of neck fur, but there was something of similarity in the sturdy golden fawn body and the wrinkled dark mass with its upturned nose and big dark eyes. Moreover it was the kind of gift that a gentleman might perfectly properly bestow upon a lady to whom he was not linked by kinship. Remembering what Russet had said of her reluctance to give up the pup, Mr Cameron thought that the little china dog might make an acceptable parting gift. For on the ride to Southampton he had forced himself to face the truth. There could be no more putting off. Indeed he should have let her go as soon as he had recognised her true quality. Today's abortive visit had been quite unnecessary.

He was pleased to discover that the little dog was quite shockingly expensive. It was of Chinese origin, the proprietor explained, very old and very rare. But for the fact that it was one of a pair and that its mate was missing, it would have been even more costly. Mr Cameron was so far gone in love that he found something singularly appropriate in the little creature's bereft state. He bought it and had it carefully wrapped, charging the shopkeeper, on an afterthought, to inform him if ever he chanced to come across the missing figure, and went back to the Dolphin foolishly comforted by the little bundle in his pocket. At least she should take something of his giving when he was obliged to let her go.

Russet stretched out on her 'doolie', as Ahmed Khan called it, in blissful relaxation. It was a very comfortable reclining chair, half palanquin, half litter, just the thing for sitting comfortably in a garden. So comfortable, in fact, that she dropped into the kind of light slumber in which familiar sounds reach the ears to be recognised and ignored. She roused to the sound of hoofs on the drive and sat up disbelievingly. It could not be so late as *that*! The foreshortened shadows of the trees confirmed her in this belief. Then she realised that she could hear carriage wheels as well as hoofs. Still drowsy and relaxed, she wondered why Mr Cameron, who had ridden out on Golden Emperor, should have chosen to hire a carriage for his return. With an anxious thump of the heart she hoped that no accident had befallen him. But the vehicle which at that moment turned the corner of the drive and bowled gently towards her was not at all the kind of thing that a gentleman would hire. It was a sober landau such as dowagers favoured, the top firmly closed despite the summer heat. And the astonished face that stared at Russet in startled recognition through the tightly closed windows was the pink and white countenance of Letty Waydene. Russet was vaguely aware that there were other occupants in the carriage, but had no time to identify them before it swung away from her as it turned to approach the main entrance.

She was granted a few moments' respite in which to shake off the last veils of sleep and brace herself to face the threatening danger. Letty had certainly recognised her, so denials or evasion would only serve to strengthen the suspicion that there was something clandestine and probably shameful about her presence. She profoundly hoped that Ahmed Khan would have the good sense to realise this. And her faith was justified. The butler presently bowed before her, his countenance imperturbable as ever, his voice gravely concerned as he said, "Three visitors, mistress. Two ladies say they know you. Miss Ingram, they say. I put gentleman in library, wait till master come home, but two ladies wish to speak you."

Russet drew a deep breath and managed a smile for him. "I rather thought I recognised them," she said tranquilly. "Well I am scarcely dressed for receiving callers but you may bring them out here to me. Set chairs for them if you please, and ask Phoebe to have tea and cakes sent out for us. You will offer the gentleman some suitable refreshment, will you not?"

Ahmed Khan bowed and withdrew. Russet planned swiftly. She refused to demean herself by lying to the Waydenes, but if prevarication would serve she must do her possible to keep them from the truth. Not only her own reputation was at stake. There was Joanna's future to be considered and the part played by Mr Cameron to be concealed. While it would do him no harm to be discovered dallying with the fashionable Miss Ingram, it would not do for any rumours of abduction to be set abroad. Russet could well imagine the reactions of some of her court. Those two foolish boys, for instance, who had so nearly come to blows over a dropped rose. Mr Cameron's existence would be rendered unsupportable by attempts to thrust duels upon him; his departure to the Highlands would be construed as flight.

But the expressions on the faces of the two ladies whom Ahmed Khan presently conducted out on to the terrace might have intimidated the boldest. Letty had dropped all pretence since there was no one at hand to be impressed. Curiosity, malice, even a hint of triumph, were all plain to be seen. Mrs Waydene's advance was militant but tempered with discretion. If there was any scandal afoot she would ferret it out with avidity, but Miss Ingram was a young woman of some consequence. If she was unjustly maligned there would be repercussions. Mrs Waydene would reconnoitre very cautiously before she brought up her heavy guns, but she commenced harrassing fire with her first words.

"So it really *is* you, Miss Ingram. I declare I could scarce believe it when Letty said she had seen you sitting here on the terrace and looking so very much at home. I had thought you—if I had thought about it at all—in Rome with your Papa by now. Was not that your intention when last we talked of our plans for the summer?"

Russet busied herself with seeing the ladies comfortably established out of the sun's glare. "It was indeed," she agreed with a rueful little smile. "But the best laid plans, ma'am, as the Scottish poet tells us–"

She let the sentence trail off as she asked if Mrs Waydene would like another cushion. That lady declined the suggestion frigidly, but was then obliged to suspend hostilities while Ahmed Khan and one of the little Indian maids arranged the tea table. She was even obliged to accept a subtle reverse when the butler gravely enquired if *she* would dispense the tea or if she wished him to do so. Russet took heart. If this was Ahmed Khan's approach, she need not fear betrayal from the servants.

Mrs Waydene poured the tea and returned to the attack. "And pray what mischance befell that you were unable to keep to your plans?" she enquired sweetly.

Russet smiled back. "An accident to my carriage," she explained. "Oh no, nothing serious. We went into the ditch to avoid a collision. My coachman went to the nearest house to get help–to pull us out of the ditch, you know–and the nearest house was this one. Only I very foolishly fainted from the shock, and when I came to myself, my maid informed me that Mr Cameron, with whom I was slightly acquainted, had insisted that I rest here until I was quite recovered."

"Dear me. And when did this accident occur?"

"Why—I suppose it must have been about eleven o'clock," returned Russet innocently. "We lay overnight at Petersfield, you see, so as to have plenty of time for the loading of the carriage."

That was sufficiently vague, she hoped, guiltily aware that it was also deliberately misleading. But it was a pity that she had chosen to wear the cream Swiss. She had done so, of course, hoping to prove to Mr Cameron that even a slender scrap like herself was not wholly devoid of femininity. But its every ruffle and fold bespoke a lady taking her afternoon ease on a summer's day in her own garden. It certainly did not suggest an earnest traveller delayed by accident.

Fortunately Mrs Waydene was pursuing another line of thought. "That heathen looking creature said that his master was gone into Southampton on business," she said sourly. "Is that in fact the case?"

Russet feigned mild bewilderment. "Why—I believe so. I rather fancy some such engagement was mentioned." And then, embroidering the lily, "You are not to be thinking him neglectful of my welfare. There was no need for him to be dancing attendance on me here, you know. I have my maid with me, and in any case I am perfectly recovered."

"Just when he was urgently needed to sort

out the tangle of Letty's affairs," snapped Mrs Waydene, unguarded in her annoyance.

She regretted the admission as soon as it was uttered. But Russet, while curious as to precisely what sort of tangle Letty had got herself into, was too preoccupied by her own delicate manoeuvring in a sea of half-truths to take advantage of the opening. "We must just wait until he comes home," decided Mrs Waydene firmly.

But if her Mama was blind to the implications of Miss Ingram's appearance, Letty, blandly confident that her mother and her guardian between them would easily smooth out the difficulty of being promised to a second gentleman before she had disengaged herself from the first, was not. As always, she had been seized with fury by Miss Ingram's effortless perfection. There was *nothing*, not one single note of high fashion about that soft, simple gown, to give it its touch of exclusiveness. Letty knew perfectly well that that inimitable air was added by the wearer, but jealousy did not blind her to the manifest unsuitability of such a gown for travelling. Either some of Miss Ingram's baggage had been unpacked so that she could change her dress after the accident or she had been at Furze House a good deal longer than she was prepared to admit. Letty was inclined to the latter theory. She had more cause than Mama for remembering the details of Miss Ingram's plans. Had she not thought that Lucian had gone to Southampton in attendance on her? And that was more than a month past. There was some mystery here that would bear investigation, decided Letty. She said thoughtfully, "I am sure Lucian said that you were sailing for Italy at the end of June."

It was not a question, but Russet dared not ignore it. She said as lightly as possible, "Did he? Well I daresay that *was* the date I mentioned at first. But the days slip past so quickly, don't they? There was some delay over finding a suitable abigail, you must know, and then I indulged myself with a few idle days in Town. It is surprisingly pleasant to linger on there after everyone else has gone into the country or to some fashionable resort. One can stroll in the park or go shopping at one's leisure. You should try it some time."

But Letty was not to be deflected. Emboldened by this attempt at evasion she said bluntly, "Are we to take it, then, that you have been all these weeks in Town? Strolling in the park and shopping?"

Russet was, in general, a tolerant creature, but this insolence was past bearing. Her temper rose and she forgot, temporarily, the difficulties of her situation. She would have burst into impetuous speech had not Jai, at that moment, emerged from beneath the doolie where she had been taking an afternoon nap. Her unexpected appearance caused Letty to give a little shriek and spring back in alarm, conduct which encouraged the pup to bark at her delightedly, inviting her to a game of tag, and gave Russet time to recollect all the dangers of rash speech. She busied herself with restraining the pup and assuring her visitors that it was the most affectionate creature despite its ferocious appearance, hoping that the little incident had diverted Letty's mind.

Mrs Waydene said disparagingly that it seemed a very odd kind of dog for a lady to choose and that for her part she did not hold with keeping animals about one's person, but Letty, once assured that the creature would not bite her, returned immediately to the far more absorbing topic of that unaccountable gap in Miss Ingram's recital. "You did not answer my question," she reminded insistently.

Russet's brows lifted in polite enquiry. "Did I not? Was it important?" she fenced desperately.

Letty said mulishly, "I asked if we were to understand that you had been all these weeks in Town."

"And I really cannot see that Miss Ingram's whereabouts are any concern of yours," suggested an icy voice from behind Russet's chair. "I am surprised that your Mama should countenance such impertinence to a lady who is my guest."

Mr Cameron, who had made good speed in his return, being anxious to present his gift to Miss Ingram, had been met as he rode into the stable yard by a worried Ahmed Khan who had swiftly furnished him with an account of his unexpected visitors. Cursing the mischance that had brought them at so inconvenient a juncture of his affairs, Mr Cameron had made haste to the rescue. Letty's remark had shown him the extreme delicacy of the situation. Characteristically he made a prompt decision.

Leaving Mrs Waydene and her daughter to swallow his rebuke with what grace they could muster, he turned to Russet. "That wretched pup has pulled your shoe-string loose *again*," he said, in a voice so different from the one he had used to Letty that all three ladies stared. "Let me tie it for you, or you may trip and fall."

He dropped lightly on one knee beside her, his back to the visitors, concealing the fact that her shoe-string was perfectly secure, and made pretence of re-fastening it. That done, he rose, sketched her a teasing mockery of a very grand bow and lightly kissed her hand, bestowing such a significant squeeze on the fingers that he held that a far slower wit than Russet's must have perceived that he was engaging her co-operation in whatever he might choose to say or do. Then he turned and smiled quite charmingly at Mrs Waydene.

"Forgive me, ma'am, if I sounded a little severe. The young are frequently careless of the appearance that they present, but I had certainly expected that Letty, with you to guide her, would have been well aware that the expression of open curiosity is only permissible in children. Since I understand that she hopes shortly to become a married lady"—he smiled, as though the thought was amusing—"she must submit herself to the code of the grown-up world." And he bestowed a forgiving smile on Letty, who stood too much in awe of him to pout and sulk as she would have liked to do.

Mrs Waydene said swiftly, "Yes, well, that is just why we are come to consult with you. About Letty's betrothal. Though it seems that we have chosen an inconvenient time." This last with a venomous glance at Russet. "Perhaps Miss Ingram would allow us to be private with you for a while. One cannot be discussing such intimate affairs in front of strangers."

"No, indeed," agreed Mr Cameron cordially. "Shocking bad ton. But you must not be regarding Russet as a stranger, you know. We have not announced it publicly since we plan to have a very quiet ceremony, but I know I can rely upon *you* to keep my confidence and need not hesitate to tell so old a friend that Miss Ingram and I are shortly to be wed. Indeed"—Mr Cameron did not disdain to tell a thumping lie in a good cause—"you behold a very disappointed man. I have just been to the receiving office hoping that our special license might have arrived, but it has not. I think I shall post off to Town myself to see if I cannot hurry matters along, once I have escorted you safely back to the Sheridans', my dear."

It was perhaps fortunate for Mr Cameron's deception that the Waydene ladies were too shocked by this disclosure to pay any attention to Russet's reactions. Letty was of the disposition that must always repine to hear that another girl was to make an advantageous marriage, and in this particular case she had a personal interest. Though the possibility had only been hinted in the most delicate way, she and her mother were of the opinion that her guardian, having attained the vast age of thirty five without showing the slightest sign of interest in females, was now unlikely to marry. In such a case, how better could he dispose of his considerable fortune than by leaving it to the family of his old friend? So Letty was furious, and hard put to it to contain her feelings. Mrs Waydene was sour and disappointed but thankful that she had been wary in her approach to the prospective bride. If she had not been particularly civil, at least she had not been openly rude. For where Miss Ingram had been a force to reckon with, Mrs Cameron would be far more formidable.

In that first moment of disclosure both ladies were too preoccupied with their own feelings to spare a glance for Russet. For Russet, who, for that one ridiculous unguarded moment had thought him serious; whose face had been irradiated by sheer ecstasy. So close they had grown, she dreamed, the understanding between them so simple and perfect, that he had not even thought it necessary to ask her consent. And then she recalled that significant pressure on her fingers; the intent, conspiratorial gleam in the dark-fringed grey eyes; and knew, with a sense of bitter desolation that this was only a play; designed, it was true, by his chivalry to protect her good name, but just make-believe in which she was expected to play her part. Valiantly she put on a smiling countenance and an air of pretty modesty almost worthy of Letty as she received their exclamations and their conventional good wishes.

Her newly acquired betrothed, well aware of the strain in her manner, sought successfully to divert the attention of the ladies to their own affairs.

"But you wished to discuss Letty's betrothal; not mine," he recalled, with that delightful, fugitive smile. "Pray forgive me! So Staneborough has come up to scratch at last, has he, Letty? And you wish me to talk with him about settlements and marriage plans."

From a man who knew perfectly well that it was not Staneborough but Robert Dysart who was nervously awaiting his arrival in the library, this was less than kind. But there was a score to be paid. Mr Cameron was not a man who liked being tricked and fooled—and Letty, with her innocent face, her practised cajolery and her deceitful tongue had fooled him to the top of his bent. So much he might have forgiven—or rather, ignored, deeming her beneath contempt now that he had her measure. But in doing so she had wrecked his hopes of happiness—for who knew how Miss Ingram might have regarded his suit if he had been given the opportunity of meeting her on fair terms—and worst of all, had caused his little love to suffer all the pains of abduction and imprisonment. Whenever he thought of that perilous attempt at escape, he still sickened. He did not attempt to minimise his own responsibility. His punishment was heavy, but he acknowledged that it was just. And Miss Letty should not escape scot free.

But by the time that she and her Mama had stumbled and stammered their way to a quite unnecessary explanation, he was feeling slightly ashamed, and went off to interview the latest aspirant to Letty's hand in a much softened frame of mind, though determined that this time he would make sure that the troublesome chit was shifted off his hands for good and all. Since the two ladies were left to the ministrations of the tender-hearted Russet, who could not help pitying their discomfort however thoroughly she disliked the pair of them, it was a reasonably contented trio who presently drove away from Furze House, waved off by the engaged couple with polite promises of future meetings and of prompt attention to such matters of business as were proper between guardian and bridegroom-elect.

Only then, in the soreness of her heart and her fierce determination that he should not guess it, did Russet turn to her quondam jailer and say briskly, "And here's a fine set-out! How do you propose to get yourself out of *that* fix? That pretty pair will have the news of our 'betrothal' spread half over Hampshire before nightfall. Your old friends whom you can trust to keep your confidence!"

Had he half hoped for a different, a gentler response? Certainly the hint of amusement that he imagined in the cool voice stung that touchy pride of his. He swallowed the humble, apologetic explanation that he had intended and smiled down at her, tall, lazily relaxed, idly stirring the squirming bull pup with his toe. "But my dear Miss Ingram," he said gently. "Whatever gave you the notion that I wished to get out of it?"

Chapter Ten

"But my dear girl! You must see that it is the only way in which I can make amends for the injury I have done you."

Russet nodded wearily. She was pale but composed, though strain had drawn dark circles beneath her eyes. "Yes. And *you* in turn, might pay some heed to my objections. I am sure your chivalry is admirable. But no woman wishes to marry simply to satisfy a man's sense of obligation."

"What will you do if you persist in your refusal to marry me? The Waydenes will undoubtedly spread the word of our betrothal, as you yourself declared, and if no marriage ensues they are bound to recollect the compromising situation in which they discovered you. I might buy their silence with the promise of a handsome dower for Letty and the other girls but one could never rely on them. Either from malice or from carelessness they might let slip some hint—and you *have* been absent from all your usual haunts for several weeks. Scandal would find ample breeding ground in that alone. At best your reputation would be sadly blown upon, your social pre-eminence at an end."

"It's little I should care for that," she retorted. And, at his raised brows, "Oh—the loss of my good name I must naturally regret. Especially as it is wholly undeserved," she threw in bitterly, hard driven by his persistence. "But social success I hold pretty cheap. It may be achieved by any oddity who chances to catch the fancy of a set of people bored to distraction by their own idleness. It very soon palls. In fact I had already made up my mind to retire from the social scene before your advent into my affairs."

"I think you under-rate yourself, child. And it is only your kind heart that prompts you to make light of your difficult position. But you have not answered me. If you will not marry me, what *will* you do?"

"I shall join Papa in Rome," she returned promptly, for it would not do to seem at a loss. "It is only until Joanna is safely married, you know. Then I can return to England and live retired in some quiet spot where no one knows me. It should be easy to make Papa's health the reason for my prolonged sojourn abroad, for his constitution was never robust and his earlier excesses"—She blushed, and falted into silence. The trouble with talking to James—to Mr Cameron—was that it was all too easy to say just what came into one's head, regardless of convention.

He ignored the impropriety. "Sentencing yourself to a living death," he said morosely, "and all to be set to my account. If you were determined on revenge, Miss Ingram, you must be satisfied that you have it now."

She was silent. She did not want revenge of course. She wanted nothing so much as to say yes to his offer. But only if he loved and wanted *her*, not because in common decency he had been obliged to make it. And they had gone over it all again and again until she was unutterably weary. So she let the accusation pass unchallenged. If he thought so poorly of her it might lessen his burden of guilt. But not even to ease his conscience would she consent to a loveless marriage. Spinster boredom would be more bearable.

Unfortunately Mr Cameron was not a man to give up easily, especially when inclination chimed so sweetly with duty. He said, though with painful diffidence, "I would ask nothing of you that you did not choose to give. And if it is the prospect of living in Scotland that is unacceptable to you, I will abandon the scheme. I ask only that you should consent to bear my name."

It was no small sacrifice. Perhaps he was not so deeply attached to the home of his ancestors as his father and his grandfather had been, yet he had planned to build his life around the bringing of fresh health and vigour to their deserted holdings. But while Russet appreciated the cost of the gesture, the thought of a marriage in name only was painful beyond endurance.

She said quietly, "If I were your wife I would wish to go to Scotland with you; to share the task with all its difficulties, its duties and its rewards. But I will not marry without love. And you, when you have a little recovered from your orgy of guilt, will remember that the House of Cameron will need an heir to ensure that the good work goes on, and will not speak so irresponsibly of marriage or of your chosen work."

In the face of such stern rebuke he could only bow that proud head and submit. He said slowly, "Very well. Will you at least permit me to charge myself with the conduct of your journey to Rome? I would like to see you safely lodged with your father, and myself explain to him the reason for the delay in your arrival. Who knows," he added with a wry little smile that tugged at her heart, "what dangers you might encounter on even so simple a journey?"

It meant that their final leave-taking would be painfully protracted, but if it would bring him some measure of comfort she would not refuse.

"*That* offer I will accept most gratefully," she said gently, "and shall be thankful to leave all the arrangements in such capable hands."

"On the principle of setting a thief to catch a thief?" he mocked, and then, suddenly serious, "I beg that you will also accept this small—memento—of your recent adventures. I had intended it as a farewell gift, which, indeed, it is. You could not take Jai to Italy, you know. Even if I gave her to you—and I should be reluctant to give up my own memento of our acquaintance—she could never endure the heat of August in those climes. This little beast"—he tugged the Chinese dog from his pocket—"will accept any climatic changes with true Oriental imperturbability. And I hope you will catch the fleeting resemblance that caused me to buy it."

She looked down at the quaint little figure, her eyes blurred by helpless tears. Why could he not have loved her? Others had done so. But the one to whom she had given her heart could give her only kindness in return. She murmured a few stumbling phrases of appreciation and thanks—she hardly knew what—and he, supposing her distress to be caused by the impending parting with her much-loved Jai, hastened to distract her thoughts by enquiring if she would, in truth, like to spend the next two nights with the Sheridans.

"They are the people at the farm," he explained, "where we buy our butter and cream. They believe themselves to be under some kind of obligation to me—quite unnecessarily. When the Furzedown estate came to be sold, the farm went with this house. I had no particular need of it, while the Sheridans had been scrimping and saving all their lives to be able to buy if the opportunity ever arose. Their gratitude over my willingness to sell to them was quite excessive. They would be only too happy to oblige me by taking you in, and I think you would be comfortable there. They are simple folk but very kind." He smiled. "And would lie valiantly in support of any tale that I chose to put about."

But Russet said that she would prefer to stay on at Furze House, making a rather feeble excuse about the nuisance of packing and unpacking for just two days. "And I could not bear to part from Phoebe before I must," she added more convincingly. And then, striving for a lighter note, "Do you know, I had it in mind from the very first to persuade Phoebe to enter my service permanently? And that I even contemplated nurturing a romance between her and Matt, not knowing they were already wed."

He smiled politely over that, then begged

her to excuse him from dining with her that night. "I must leave all my affairs in train before I escort you overseas," he explained. "If I set out for Town at once I can save a whole day."

Russet would have liked to protest. He had already ridden to Southampton that day and must be tired. Surely one day could not make so much difference. But as she had dismissed him so firmly and finally perhaps he felt some embarrassment in her society. Certainly there could be no possibility of reverting to their recent easy companionship. She resigned herself to a lonely evening.

She went early to bed and cried herself to sleep, clutching to her an unresponsive yellow china dog, precious because it was *his* gift. And as though to mark the ending of her idyll the next day brought rain, keeping her to the house, where she spent a miserable time in supervising Ameera's preparations for her departure. Only the naughtiness of Jai, lacking her usual exercise and bursting with energy and mischief, served to lighten her black depression. She kept the pup with her that night, despite Heaton's gloomy warning about pampering and Phoebe's freely expressed disapproval of dogs in bedrooms. At least it was warm and living. It leaned against her knees in a companionable way and its great dark eyes expressed dumb sympathy with her incomprehensible grief.

Next day she felt a little more cheerful. There were gleams of watery sunshine that permitted outdoor excursions for girl and pup. She even ventured to hope that Mr Cameron might have dispatched his business with unexpected rapidity and would return by nightfall. But the dinner hour came and went without any bustle of arrival. She had to content herself with the reflection that she could count upon his returning tomorrow as he himself had reckoned.

The sound of hoofs beating a rapid tattoo on the drive, long awaited, eventually took her by surprise. It was so much earlier than she had expected—barely noon. Her heart seemed to quicken its beat in sympathy with the rhythm, for there was something ominous about it. What should cause Mr Cameron, notoriously considerate of his horse, to arrive at a full gallop? Whenever they had ridden together he had been most insistent about bringing the horses in cool.

Her impatience, her sudden springing anxiety, could not be bridled by convention. She made the best speed she could to the stable yard to find out for herself. There, indeed, was a steaming, jaded horse, head a-droop. But the rider who had just flung himself from the saddle was not Mr Cameron but the groom who had gone with him, and Herrick and most of the stable staff, alarmed as Russet had been by the unusual nature of his arrival, had abandoned their duties to gather round him with anxious enquiries.

As Russet came up she heard the man say, "Warned 'im, I did, that 'twas risky, setting out so late. And now look at what's come of it. Nothing would do for 'im but to get 'ome last night. The doctor says 'e's not fit to be moved. Lorst a lot o'blood and like to be in 'igh fever by nightfall. But 'e's awake and clear in the 'ead and 'e sez 'e's going 'ome. So I've come for the carriage and Mrs 'errick, wot's better than any nurse, to go and fetch 'im."

Unconsciously Russet pressed both hands to her breast as though to subdue the agitated beating of her heart, but her voice was quiet and controlled as she stepped into the circle of listeners and said, "Something amiss? Has Mr Cameron met with an accident?"

The circle opened to admit her, the eager questioners falling silent, the groom tugging nervously at his forelock, then expanding into volubility as he temporarily forgot his genuine concern for his master in his own brief importance.

"Not to say a haccident, miss," he began. "We was set upon by 'ighwaymen. Just coming down towards Hambledon. Three of 'em, the leader yelling at us to stand and 'and over the dibs. The master was riding Flying Fox and 'e made pretence that the beast was out o' control, rearing and such, while 'e worked 'is pistol out o' the 'olster. But one o' them spotted what 'e was at and let fly. The shot took the Fox low in the neck. Then the other two joined in and there was a reg'lar flurry o' shots. I was that mazed I couldn't rightly say just 'ow it 'appened. I'd got me own barkin' iron out by then, and I reckon I winged one o' the bast- —sorry, miss, one o' them. Then the master was down, hanging over the Fox's neck and one o' the highwaymen was sprawled in the dust. The other made off, and the fellow I'd hit went after 'im. I 'ad to let 'em go 'cos I'd all on to see to the master, 'oo was bleeding like a stuck pig, and which way they went I couldn't rightly say. The poor old Fox went down and I just managed to drag the master out o' the saddle before 'e rolled over and pinned 'im. Did my best to stop the bleeding—the master, not the Fox, 'e'd gorn—but with only my shirt and neckcloth to tie 'im up with I doubt it was a botched job. 'E came to just as I was finishing and between us we managed to get 'im up on Jemima"—he nodded at his exhausted mount—"but what with leading the mare and trying to 'old 'im in the saddle, and main afraid as 'e'd break out bleeding again, I thought I'd never get 'im into shelter. And then we 'ad a stroke o' luck. A gig came down the road and overtook us, and damme if it weren't Doctor Unwin. Our own doctor, miss, as used to attend 'er ladyship. Never so glad to see 'pothecary in all my puff!"

There was a concerted sigh of relief from the attentive listeners. Herrick, irascible in his anxiety, said shortly, "Taken your time getting here, haven't you?"

"We'd to get the master to shelter first," protested the groom, "and then the doctor 'ad to get the bullet out of 'im. Seemed a long time," he muttered inadequately, recalling how the doctor had sworn at him for a clumsy oaf and bewailed aloud the fate that had directed them to a womanless household and given him a 'misbegotten moon-calf with two left feet where his hands should have been' as his sole assistant; for the schoolmaster upon whose hospitality they had thrust themselves was one that couldn't abide the sight of blood without swooning.

But despite his curses the doctor had recognised the groom's willingness and devotion. Once he had done all he could for his patient, he had not hesitated to leave the lad in charge. Mr Cameron was unlikely to rouse. If he did, he could be given the draught which the doctor would leave for him and water or tea to drink if he was thirsty. Not wine. The doctor himself must return to the patient who had called him out. For he was attending a lying-in. An awkward cross-birth, too, though the groom, with a respectful glance at Russet, did not embark on these intimate details at this point. He must get back at once, but as soon as the child was safely delivered and he had snatched a few hours' sleep he would return to see how Mr Cameron did.

He had done so, to find Mr Cameron conscious, though very weak, and determined to be conveyed to his own establishment without loss of time.

"And it's taken you till now to get here, even with galloping the mare into a lather?" grunted Herrick. "Lost your way, I suppose."

"I couldn't leave until the doctor gave the word," protested the lad. "And 'e said as 'ow I must go with 'im first to make a deepo—something in front of a magistrate."

"A deposition," put in Russet quietly. "Saying just what had happened, so that possibly the malefactors might be apprehended."

"That's it, miss," agreed the groom gratefully. "Though I don't know nothing about no mallyfactors. I just 'ad to say what 'appened and give my affy-davy like I was in a court o' law. But then 'e asks a lot o' questions about the b-begging your pardon, miss, about what our hassailants looked like, and that's what delayed me." This with a resentful scowl at Herrick.

"I guess you did pretty well at that," grunted that worthy. "Couldn't ha' done any better meself, though I'm downright nattered to think of such a thing happening and me not by to lend a hand." At which handsome amends the groom's expression lightened, and when Russet added gently that she thought he had done very well indeed he blushed bashfully and stammered out a few incoherent phrases about only doing his duty and the master being a great gun.

If Russet had ever wondered fleetingly in just what light Mr Cameron's servants regarded her, the next half hour provided comforting reassurance. They had always treated her with respect, but that might be only the outcome of good training–and Ahmed Khan was a stern disciplinarian. Now they turned to her–even Ahmed Khan himself–for advice and comfort. And in giving it she eased her own sore heart and stifled her fears. She would dearly have loved to go with Matt and Phoebe to bring the master home, but a moment's rational consideration showed her that there was nothing he would dislike more. To be exposing herself to public scrutiny and comment when he had been at such pains to protect her good name that he had even offered to marry her! She contented herself instead with suggesting that Herrick should try if the 'doolie' could be fitted into the coach since it would add considerably to the invalid's comfort, and with helping Phoebe to collect pillows and rugs. Benjy, the young groom, begged leave to go too, to act as guide, and though his services were quite unnecessary, Herrick, repenting of his earlier severity, assented.

In Phoebe's absence she earnestly debated invalid diets with Ahmed Khan and the cook, suggesting that chickens should be killed for the preparation of sustaining broths and the finest brandy looked out in case desperate measures were required. And in her secret heart one tiny seed of comfort grew and strengthened her. This mishap must delay her own departure. Perhaps she would be permitted to help nurse him—at least to bear him company when he was convalescent.

She would not permit her mind to dwell on any outcome other than convalescence and eventual recovery. He was in the prime of life and vigorous health. He had been singularly fortunate in receiving prompt and skilled medical attention, and if the doctor had thought his state serious he would have returned to the patient's side a good deal earlier than he had, in fact, done. It was not even as though he was a stranger. If Mr Cameron or any of his household had needed the services of a doctor, presumably it would have been Doctor Unwin who was summoned. She could be sure that her beloved had received every care and attention. Beyond that she would not think.

And perhaps—just perhaps—in his weakness and dependence, he might turn to her at last in love.

Chapter Eleven

"I cannot like it," pronounced Doctor Unwin gravely. "The inflammation has subsided and the wound is beginning to heal just as it should. But there is a lassitude that becomes alarming. One must remember that Mr Cameron has spent a good deal of his life in the Orient. There are diseases, fevers, with which we are unfamiliar. But I have heard theories that they may lie dormant in the blood for many years, only to become active and virulent when the patient is weakened by some other illness or, as in this case, by loss of blood."

Russet and Phoebe, who had shared the nursing, nodded sober understanding. The doctor, delighted to have so intelligent and cooperative an audience, proceeded to enlarge on his theme.

"In such a case it is of the first importance to build up the patient's strength and to keep up his spirits. For the first we may rely upon suitable nourishment and the healing power of sleep. At the moment it is the second which is causing me concern. As a man of science I do not subscribe to superstition. I am no believer in evil omens and premonitions. But Mr Cameron's preoccupation with the orderly arrangement of his worldly affairs appears to me to be morbid. It is the only matter to which he has given a thought since he was brought—much against my advice—back to Furze House. Indeed, the only occasion upon which I have seen him show signs of animation was when his attorney was announced."

"I believe him to be anxious to complete the purchase of an estate in Scotland," offered Russet tentatively.

The doctor shook his head. "That may be so. But on this occasion he made no secret of the fact that it was the drawing of a new Will that concerned him. That, and the arrival of some document that he had instructed his attorney to procure for him. *Not* a healthy attitude. A man may change his Will if he so chooses. But to be doing so when he is lying on a sick bed is depressing to the spirits and not to be encouraged. If he was at death's door it would be understandable, but until this strange fancy took possession of his mind he was making good progress."

He then enquired as to the patient's appetite

and how he was sleeping, shook his head over the information that the ladies gave, and said that he would call again next day, when he trusted that they would be able to give him a better report.

Left alone, the pair exchanged miserable glances.

"Never ate a morsel of that beautiful fresh sole," said Phoebe despairingly. "And Benjy riding all that way special. Not to mention Cook making a white wine sauce to poach it in that was so smooth you'd think it 'ud have tempted anybody. Oh, Miss Russet, I'm sore afraid he's made up his mind to die." And she put her head down on Russet's breast, her body shaking with sobs that she tried in vain to control.

Russet did her best to pour scorn on so ridiculous a notion. People couldn't just give up trying and decide that they would die, she said stoutly. But she had grave misgivings herself. She had sat with the invalid all afternoon while Phoebe snatched some much needed sleep. He had not once spoken, although she knew very well that he had not been asleep. Looking down at him, so suggestively still under the light coverlets that were all that his wound would endure, he had put her strongly in mind of the effigy of a crusader that she had once seen on a tomb in some churchyard. Even to the dog, couched at his feet. For Jai, apparently understanding the needs of a sick-room despite her youth, had mourned noisily and persistently until admitted at Mr Cameron's own feebly-voiced request, whereupon she had mouthed a lax hand and subsided into silent watchfulness at the foot of the bed. She gave no trouble so long as she was allowed to remain on guard, and left the room only for food and exercise at Russet's insistence, returning eagerly to her self-appointed post as soon as the door was opened.

She had gazed at him with a heart full of love, and of pity for his weakness, but there had been apprehension, too. An apprehension born of that macabre resemblance. And now that apprehension was painfully possessive. She did not know a great deal about nursing, but it was only common sense to accept that a man who had lost a great deal of blood needed nourishment. Dr Unwin had ordered a light diet—no red meats or heavy wines—but he was obviously concerned about the patient's loss of appetite. Russet was inclined to respect his judgement. Even when Mr Cameron had been feverish he had refused to bleed him, saying that he had lost blood enough already. That, too, seemed to be common sense. So when Dr Unwin admitted to concern, Russet was all the more anxious.

She passed a restless night, and her anxieties were in nowise allayed when admission to the sick-room next morning revealed little change in the patient's condition. If anything the arrogant nose and chin seemed more prominent, the cheeks more sunken, the breathing shallower. He had been washed and shaved by his Indian body-servant—who spoke no English, so could not report on his master's state—and the clean, uncreased bed-linen added to the corpse-like effect.

Russet shivered. She wanted to sob and scream, but what good would that do? Instead she seated herself in the low chair beside the bed and set slim fingers on his wrist. She thought his pulse was more rapid but was too inexperienced to be sure.

Perhaps the soft touch had roused him; perhaps he had been awaiting her coming. At any rate he turned his head a little on the pillow and smiled at her. "Rosetta," he pronounced softly.

She was startled. It was very rare for anyone to address her by her given name. She remembered that during the intimacy of that friendship that now seemed a lifetime away, he had once commented on the appropriate nature of her name. She had confided that Mama had had her christened Rosetta. It was Papa, seeing the coppery hue of the toddling babe's curls, who had called her Russet. What strange quirk of a sick man's fancy had recalled that small unimportant incident?

She smiled down at him, and since his eyes remained open began to talk gently of small familiar things as the doctor had advised, telling him that it was another lovely day and that she and Jai had walked in the wild garden before breakfast and the pup had met her first hedgehog. Presently invention failed and she fell silent, studying the strong, capable hand that now lay so limp and quiet on the sheet. Even after only a week the sun tan was already fading. As she gazed, his eyes opened again and the hand moved a little towards her, turning palm upward, so that instinctively she put her own into it. His fingers closed over hers. He said again, "Rosetta. My attorney is coming this afternoon. Will you come, too, please, while he is here?"

Even that small effort seemed to exhaust him. The fingers clasping hers relaxed their hold, the heavy lids closed. She said easily, "Of course. But I, too, have a request to make. If you are to be talking business this afternoon, will you not at least *try* to take some nourishment first?"

He did not answer directly. "Don't fret that tender heart of yours over me, child," he said gently. "Unwin has promised me a cordial that he says will enable me to complete the business that I have in mind. That is all that matters."

Words of indignant reproach trembled on her lips, but he looked so unutterably weary that she restrained herself. She said instead, "I myself have made the chicken broth that you are to have for your luncheon, risking Cook's wrath to do so. It is from a recipe that Mama taught me, and she was used to enjoy it when she could fancy nothing else. It would please me very much if you would be persuaded to try it."

His lips curved to a faint smile but he did not speak and she did not like to press him further.

It was a distinct shock to discover, when Ahmed Khan summoned her to the sick-room that afternoon, that there were at least half a dozen people gathered there, and that several of them were strangers. Dr Unwin made her known to Mr Anderson, the attorney, and to a homely looking middle-aged couple who turned out to be Mr and Mrs Sheridan. The senior members of the domestic staff were there, in addition to Phoebe and Matt. Mr Cameron was propped up with pillows in a half sitting position which Russet thought most injudicious since the doctor had, throughout, insisted that he lie as flat as possible, permitting only one thin pillow. But there was a trace of colour in his cheeks and he looked more his usual self. The result of the doctor's cordial no doubt, thought Russet bitterly, and at what cost in exhaustion when its effect wore off? The thought crossed her mind that if she had accepted that offer of marriage she would now have been in a position to veto such folly. But small use to think of that at this juncture. She crossed to the window and seated herself inconspicuously, as she hoped, beside Phoebe.

Apparently her coming completed the company, for Mr Anderson, refreshing his memory by glancing from time to time at a slip of paper in his hand, began to explain why they had been invited to be present. This duty he had taken upon himself in order to spare Mr Cameron's strength, he said. Russet looked at him more approvingly.

His client, he continued, having no surviving blood kin so far as he was aware, had made testamentary dispositions which would provide for his household according to age and the length of time that they had been in his service. He himself was charged with the responsibility of helping the younger servants to find suitable employment and of making travelling arrangements for such of the Indian staff as wished to return to their own country. There would be life pensions and legacies in certain cases. The general burden of his remarks was that, however Mr Cameron's present illness should terminate, none of his servants need feel any anxiety for the future.

There was a tearing sob from Phoebe. Russet, her own throat raw with tears, squeezed her hand comfortingly.

The Sheridans, it appeared, were there to

witness the signing of the Will and to hear what Mr Cameron had to say to his friends and neighbours.

That seemed to conclude Mr Anderson's part in the proceedings, for, with a nice attention to the proper disposition of his coat tails, he seated himself beside the bed.

There was an awkward little silence. No one knew quite what to do. Should they voice their gratitude now? Was the interview ended? Only Russet, her senses alert for any change, any weakness that might show in the invalid's manner, noticed the hands that gripped the folded-back sheet with a tension that whitened the knuckles, and longed to interfere—to send them all away. It should never have been allowed. He was driving himself to his death.

Yet his voice struck clearly in her ears. More serious than was his wont, he spoke very simply.

"Those of you who have come here this afternoon at my request are the people who know me best of anyone in this country. I have tried to be a fair master to my servants and to deal honestly with my friends. Today I ask your help. Not for myself, but for one who is very dear to me." A pause here, as though he gathered his forces to continue. "Had matters fallen out otherwise," he went on slowly, "it had been my dearest wish to have made her my wife. Since that is not possible, I have bequeathed to her the residue of my fortune."

There was a long pause here. Russet struggled with a nightmare sense of unreality. He *could* not be talking about her!

The weary voice from the bed took up its theme again. "In such a case, as you well know, malice and jealousy often breed scandal, and so I most particularly wish all in this room to know the true facts, and, should it be necessary, to support and comfort Miss Ingram."

This time there was amazement as well as sorrow in the tense silence. It was broken by Bob Sheridan who said bluntly, "I'm sure Mary and me'll do all as we can to help the young lady and main glad to do it. But you shouldn't be talking as though you was booked, sir. There's many a man worse wounded than you was that's still living hearty, and with so pretty a lady promised to you"—he glanced at Russet in apology for the familiarity—"you've the best in life ahead. Maybe we'll all dance at your wedding yet."

There were murmurs and nods of assent all round the room, and one or two sympathetic glances for Russet. It was natural that the listeners should have misunderstood the situation, she thought. James had spoken of his desire to marry her. He had not mentioned her rejection. And comforting as it was to see the shy friendliness on the faces turned to her, she writhed with distaste at the falseness of her position. Quite irrationally she was suddenly furiously angry. Let himself die, would he? Like some sickly love-lorn loon in an old romance. Burden her with his money and leave her to live out a life of lonely regret for the might-have-been. They would see about that.

Resolutely she swallowed her wrath until the last of the servants had left, bade the Sheridans a friendly farewell and listened courteously to the doctor's parting instructions that the patient must now be permitted to rest. As he and Mr Anderson took their leave she advanced upon the bed, hands on hips, eyes blazing, a veritable virago. Rest indeed! Not until she had given him a piece of her mind!

"So that is how a Highland gentleman shuffles off his responsibilities," she raged at him. "You'll fold your hands and give yourself up to death, will you? And think that makes all smooth. I don't want your odious money. If you insist on dying despite me, I'll give it to the Foundling Hospital. But you're not going to die, because I won't let you. Two of us can wallow in orgies of guilt. Since you were travelling for my service when you were wounded, why should I not hold myself responsible for your state? Am I to suffer remorse for that all my days? You are going to get better, James Cameron, and you're going to begin now."

The grey eyes regarded her steadily. There was no weariness in the voice now as he said, "Such concern would be becoming in a wife. But you are not my wife. Since you would have none of me, *I* will have none of your concern."

She would not draw back now. "Very well," she said curtly. "If you still wish it, I will marry you. But I warn you it's a sorry bargain you're making."

He actually managed a faint grin, with something of his old teasing air. "I am aware. It's a red-headed vixen that I'm taking to wife. But only in name. That was the bargain and I hold by it. I said I would ask no more of you. If you choose to nurse me—or was it rather scold me—back to health, then you may pride yourself on being the more generous party."

She nodded. "Agreed. You may send for your special license—and I will plan my campaign."

Miss Ingram departed with dignity and a certain sense of triumph. Mr Cameron turned rather gingerly on his side—his wound really *was* rather troublesome still—and slipped one hand under his pillow. He pulled out a paper and unfolded it carefully. It was a licence for a marriage between James Ewan Cameron and Rosetta Caroline Ingram. He read it through yet again and tucked it away with a contented smile. He should, he supposed, be feeling thoroughly ashamed of himself. To be sure he had not contrived the hold-up nor deliberately courted injury. The devotion with which Russet had tended him during the first days of his helplessness was surely evidence that she had *some* liking for him, and she did not love anyone else. He had her own word for that. Very well. So he had deceived her. But if a little play acting could win him his wife, then he would woo her as never a girl was wooed before, once she was safely his. The grief that he had caused his well-wisher did cost him a few twinges of guilt. He could only hope that it would be assuaged by his rapid recovery.

He settled himself for a nap. He was still damnably weak, though that was largely his own fault, starving himself in furtherance of his base plot. Some day he would have to confess his duplicity, but that day was far off. Meanwhile he would gratify his fierce little nurse by displaying meek obedience and a rapidly improving appetite.

Chapter Twelve

"Wife," said Mr Cameron, secretly savouring the word.

Russet paid no heed.

"Woman," said her lord and master. "Come and amuse me. I am bored to distraction with my own society."

"When you were a very small boy," said his wife in affable enquiry, "did anyone ever teach you to say please?"

He chuckled. "Yes. But I am no longer a small boy. And when you became a wife, five days ago, did you not solemnly promise to obey me?"

She looked up indignantly at that. They were sitting on the terrace once again. This time it was Mr Cameron who was stretched at ease in the 'doolie' while Russet was struggling with the composition of a letter to her father which would apprise him of her new state.

"A wife in name only," she reminded him.

But she put her letter aside and came to sit beside him. "What would you like to do?" she invited. "A hand of piquet? I shall never be able to give you a game of chess—I just haven't got the right kind of mind. Or do you feel equal to another turn about the garden?"

They had been married just two days after Russet had so ungraciously given her consent. He had not dared to strain her credulity by producing the licence any sooner. They had planned a very quiet ceremony in the village church with only Matt and Phoebe to serve as witnesses, but the secret leaked out, as it was bound to do, since arrangements had to be made for the bridegroom to be helped to his place and for a chair to be placed at the Chancel steps, as he would be obliged to remain seated during most of the ceremony. Mr Cameron, who would have preferred to present a dignified, if not precisely a gallant figure at his nuptials, decided philosophically that it served him right for his underhanded manoeuvring. It also had the advantage of causing his bride to gaze at him with an anxious tenderness that brought sentimental tears to Phoebe's eyes and revived the bridegroom's hopes that in time his wife might come to like him pretty well.

These had been slightly dashed during the two days that had elapsed since their betrothal. Her manner had been cool and astringent—the behaviour of a firm but kindly nurse towards a wayward child who must be checked and controlled for his own good. She had been very quiet and sober, too. No jokes, or teasing. He was possessed by fears that even at the last moment she might change her mind and was thankful indeed to see her come slowly up the aisle with Phoebe. The little church was surprisingly full. The combination of a wounded bridegroom and a mysterious bride whom few people had seen had caught the imagination of the village. Most of the domestic staff were there—he had not thought to forbid them—and the Sheridans and several of his farmer friends and their families as well as Anderson to see the knot firmly tied. The doctor, too, had insisted that his support was necessary, and so, in fact it was. But once the service began Mr Cameron forgot all about the minor intrusion of the watching faces and the indignities forced upon him by physical weakness. He listened humbly, with a prayer for forgiveness if he had done wrong, and made his vows with quiet sincerity. Only once was there a slight confusion. As the bridegroom repeated the words, 'to have and to hold' he gripped the slender hand that had just been placed in his so fiercely that Russet involuntarily winced and gasped, causing the diffident little priest, already slightly disconcerted by the unusual circumstances and the presence of Ahmed Khan, awesome in spotless robes of ceremony and intricate turban, to falter and lose his place. But habit reasserted itself and in a moment he went steadily on, "From this day forward."

The ceremony ended, they received the good wishes of their friends in rather subdued fashion, Russet obviously anxious that her husband's strength should not be overtaxed. Bob Sheridan reminded them jovially that he had foretold what would happen, though he certainly had not looked to see it happen so soon, and Mr Cameron regretted that Bob would not be able to *dance* at his wedding but promised that there should be a suitable celebration as soon as he was fully recovered. At this point Doctor Unwin, who seemed to have taken upon himself most of the duties of groom's man, pointed out that the carriage was waiting to carry the bridal pair back to Furze House.

The serious mood in which the drive was accomplished was dispelled over luncheon when the bridegroom insisted that they should pledge each other in champagne, but this assertion of authority was short-lived. As soon as the meal was over his wife ordained that he must rest after the exertions of the morning. Mr Cameron, a little amused by this display of conjugal behaviour, was willing to humour her—and horrified when he awoke to find that the afternoon was already far advanced. He was, however, permitted to come downstairs again for dinner, and even to indulge in a rubber of piquet. But his suggestion that his wife, who had won handsomely, should give him an opportunity for revenge was firmly vetoed. He was reminded that he was still an invalid and ordered back to bed. To speak truth he was thankful enough to get between sheets, and when Russet came in presently with a milk posset that she insisted upon his drinking, he won a chuckle from her by informing her that getting married was an exhausting business and that he could only be grateful to her for not subjecting him to all the flummery of a fashionable wedding. Despite his fatigue he looked a little better, she thought, and oddly boyish as he wrinkled his nose in disgust over the posset. She would dearly have loved to lean over and drop a kiss on his cheek but she reminded herself briskly of the terms of their bargain. He did not love her. Her caresses could only embarrass him.

They settled back easily enough into a semblance of the easy intercourse which had been so abruptly terminated by the visit from the Waydenes. There could be no riding, of course, but Mr Cameron, making rapid progress under his wife's watchful eye, was soon well enough to be driven out for an hour or so when the weather was propitious. He grumbled a good deal about the restrictions that she imposed on his activities, and assured her that if he had known what it was like to live under the cat's foot he would have thought twice about marrying her. All he got by that was a calm reminder that he had been given fair warning.

"I told you I was a bad bargain. And I daresay it is doing you a great deal of good to have that imperious will of yours overborne from time to time. I mean to make the most of my opportunities while you are too weak to resist, or you will be quite impossible to live with."

His plan to woo his wife by every subtle means that he could devise made no progress at all. While talk ran on practical day to day affairs they got on splendidly, usually agreeing, sometimes arguing amiably and coming to a satisfactory compromise. But as soon as any topic of a personal or intimate nature crept in, Russet became evasive. In those delightful early days they had enjoyed exploring each other's minds and tastes, delving into childish memories and comparing prejudices. Nowadays conversation was confined to items of local interest, to consideration of whether or no Mr Cameron would be well enough to escort his wife to Denholme for her sister's wedding in October, and discussion of the re-decoration of Russet's 'prison' in a fashion more suited to a younger woman. For as she had suspected the room had been his mother's and had been furnished in accordance with her tastes. This particular topic, together with a running battle over the laying out of the flower borders for next season, was about the nearest that they approached to marital intimacy. The new Mrs Cameron had fitted so easily into her rôle as châtelaine of Furze House that she had a dozen reasons for slipping away if she felt that her husband was approaching forbidden ground. She must talk to Cook or consult Phoebe or enquire into the dealings of the hen-wife or the laundry-maids. And of course there was always Jai, who had reverted to normal puppyhood with her master's recovery, and had to be fed, exercised, scolded or entertained whenever Mr Cameron might otherwise have been able to claim his wife's undivided attention. There were moments when, in furious exasperation at his lack of progress, he could almost have wished that she was still a prisoner under lock and key. At least, then, if he desired her presence, she could not escape him. Now, although he would have had difficulty in quoting a single instance, he knew that she was eluding him in a way that was not purely physical. There was a hedge of reserve about her, more impenetrable than the thorny barrier than once guarded the sleeping princess, and try as he might he could not overcome it.

On the surface all was smooth. There were letters and calls and a visit from Cousin Olivia accompanied by Doll. The pug bullied the much larger Jai quite shamefully and Cousin

Olivia succumbed to the charm of her host, pitied his present invalidism and privately assured Russet that she was a very fortunate girl. So far as birth and fortune were concerned, not even Joanna had made a better match. To be sure he was not heir to a dukedom, but where personal attraction was in question—her delicately plucked eyebrows vanished.

But daily one enormous obstacle bulked larger and larger on Mr Cameron's horizon. What of the future? He was practically recovered from his injury, but still no decision had been made as to where they should live. Obviously they would stay at Furze House until after Joanna's wedding, but what then? The purchase of the Scottish estate had been completed. At this season of the year little could be done on the practical side, but Mr Cameron knew very well that he should take up residence as soon as possible. Getting acquainted with his tenants and his new neighbours was likely to be a long slow business; one, moreover, that could best be pursued at a time of year when they were not wholly preoccupied by seasonal tasks. Even the bitter months of winter could be turned to useful purpose, since they might permit him to relieve hardship, so that he used infinite tact and good judgement.

Russet had said, once, that if she was his wife she would wish to share the Scottish adventure with him. But it had been an academic discussion. In any case he had said that he would make no demands upon her other than that she would consent to take his name, so he could hardly ask her to go into what amounted to voluntary exile with him. Nor would it cause any particular comment if he left her comfortably established in the Town house. Society would be far more likely to smile and raise eyebrows if she went with him. He could perfectly well imagine the sly comments about newly-weds and romantic idylls.

He tried an oblique approach, asking her what she would like to do when he travelled north. Unfortunately, in his anxiety to leave her absolutely free to choose, he went on, "You could stay on here, you know, if you do not think it too isolated. The winters are quite mild as a rule. Or you could stay in Cavendish Square if you preferred it. I daresay Cousin Olivia would be quite happy to bear you company." Russet promptly decided that, honour being satisfied with giving her the protection of his name, he no longer had any particular desire for her society. She returned an indifferent answer, saying that she would think it over and perhaps consult Cousin Olivia. And for the second time during her stay at Furze House, cried herself to sleep.

Heaton met her next morning with a long face. Now that she had grown too large for a basket, Jai slept in the kennels, and it was Russet's custom to stroll down there each morning after breakfast and take her out.

"Proper sick, poor little bitch," he told her gloomily. "I doubt it's distemper, and she's got it bad."

It seemed to Russet that everything was going wrong at once. She had begun the day feeling thoroughly miserable after last night's talk with her husband and Jai's illness seemed to be the last straw. Nor had Heaton exaggerated. Even to Russet's inexperienced eyes the pup looked very ill. She lay inert on the straw, her painful breathing the only sign of life.

"Takes 'em badly, this breed," explained Heaton mournfully. He was especially fond of the lively, mischievous pup, having brought her up by hand.

He had little comfort to offer. There was not much they could do save to keep the pup warm and bathe away the mucus from her eyes and nostrils. "And try to persuade her to eat," added Heaton heavily. "That's the trouble. They won't eat. Then, by the time the fever 'bates, they're too weak to pull through. I'll do my best for her, miss—ma'am, I *should* say, but it's only straight to own that I'm not hopeful."

"Then pray don't tell the master," said Russet impulsively. "Else we shall have him down here helping to nurse her and perhaps taking cold. He is much occupied at present with business matters. He may not notice that she is not about the house."

Heaton looked doubtful, but he agreed that it wouldn't do to have the master sitting up nights with a sick animal. Russet said that she herself would help with the nursing. Heaton was dubious about that, too, but Russet was sure that if anyone could persuade Jai to lap the broth with which Heaton had been trying to tempt her, *she* could. Alas! Her efforts were no more successful than Heaton's. The pup lay like a dead thing, her glossy coat dull and harsh to the touch, not hearing their anxious voices nor responding to Russet's urging.

"Best leave her be," said Heaton finally. "I'll try again in a while. Maybe a bit o' raw liver 'ud tempt her."

Mr Cameron began to find his wife more elusive than ever. During the first weeks of their married life she had at least driven out with him most afternoons and sat with him in the library after dinner. Now she excused herself from the afternoon excursions on the lamest of excuses and would retire as soon as dinner was done, saying that she was very tired. She did *look* tired, Mr Cameron was obliged to admit, but the long nights of sleep did not appear to refresh her, for she would come down to breakfast pale and heavy-eyed still.

He began to be seriously concerned for her health. The weeks of imprisonment had made little apparent impression on her. Marriage—a marriage that was no marriage, a marriage that he had practically forced upon her—seemed to be undermining her constitution with dangerous rapidity.

She had always been slight of build, but her slenderness had been imbued with vigorous health, a vital warmth that was her greatest charm. He looked at her across the dinner table, aware that she was making only a pretence of eating, and saw the brave effort she made to smile and to converse; saw that the slight body was drooping with weariness, that there were dark circles under her eyes. And for the first time he realised the depths of his own selfishness. He had thought of her welfare, true. He had protected her reputation and dwelt joyously on the luxuries with which he would heap her. But he had thought of her happiness only in relation to himself. He had not been able to see that some other man might give her all that he could give and happiness as well. And this was what he had brought her to. In bitter self-reproach and penitence he forestalled her usual faltering excuses.

"You look very tired, my dear. I think you should go early to bed," he said. And saw the thankfulness that she could not quite hide.

He himself sat long in the library, occasionally rising to throw another log on the fire and to pace the floor in painful thought till the ache in the newly healed wound sent him back to his chair. It was long past midnight when, his hard decision reached, he summoned Jamal to help him to bed. It was even longer before sleep banished the bleak misery that engulfed him.

In the stable block the fight for Jai's life went on. They had moved her from the kennels for fear of the other dogs taking the sickness and installed her in a snug corner in the harness room. Russet had made her a kind of coat out of a blanket, and in a deep nest of straw she was protected from chills. Russet and Heaton shared the nursing between them and the pup was never left. On the third night Heaton had shaken his head hopelessly. The pup had taken nothing all day, not even water. In desperation, and with some faint recollection of her father's actions in a similar situation, Russet had called Ahmed Khan into their councils. Ahmed Khan was no dog lover—he thought them unclean beasts—but he loved his master devotedly and that devotion was rapidly spreading to include Russet. Without complaint he produced his master's finest brandy. He watched them add the golden liquid to a well-beaten egg without so much as a shudder for such desecration and even stood impassively by while the mixture was carefully coaxed down a dog's throat.

The effect was heartening. After a few moments Jai opened her eyes and even tried to raise her head. She was presently persuaded to lap feebly at a broth compounded of rabbit and chicken. No more than a few mouthfuls, but it was the first hopeful sign. Her two nurses glanced at each other with wary optimism.

"Every two hours?" suggested Russet, nodding at the brandy bottle. "And then try her with the broth or milk. Maybe with a little of the meat mixed in the broth, if its stewed to rags."

Heaton nodded sage agreement. And between them they had carried out the treatment, he bearing most of the responsibility during the day, save for a brief rest during the afternoon, Miss Russet–and he must remember to call her Mrs Cameron–taking the brunt of the night nursing. Never was a bottle of brandy mis-used to better purpose. The invalid grew stronger daily. Even Ahmed Khan took a detached but benevolent interest in her progress. And tonight, for the first time, she had struggled to her feet and devoured a small portion of sheep's liver with obvious appetite.

"She'll do," exclaimed Heaton, his face one wide, joyous grin. "She's going to do it. And it's all thanks to you, Miss Russet. Bless your bonny face and your warm heart."

He was then so overcome by the familiarity into which his feelings had betrayed him that he hastily mumbled something about seeing if

Bob Sheridan could get a couple more rabbits for them and stumped off before Russet could express her thanks for *his* patient care, which had done quite as much for Jai as she had.

She sat on beside the sleeping pup, utterly weary but at peace. She even dozed a little from time to time, no longer obsessed by the fear that Jai would die while she slept. Heaton relieved her at five o'clock and she stole back softly to the side door that Ahmed Khan had left unlocked for her. Breakfast was not until nine so she could surrender to the overpowering urge to relax and sleep in the comfort of a proper bed.

Not unnaturally she overslept and did not even rouse when Ameera came in with her hot water. She was late for breakfast. Her husband had finished his meal and was getting up as she came in. She apologised for her tardy arrival and he said gravely that he hoped she felt the better for her long sleep.

"I would be grateful if you could spare me a few moments when you have done your breakfast," he added. "There is something I wish to discuss with you. Perhaps you will come to me in the library when you are at liberty."

She nodded acquiescence and poured herself some coffee. She was not particularly hungry and contented herself with a slice of bread and butter, too tired to serve herself from the several delectable dishes that Cook had sent up, wishing only that she could go back to bed and sleep for a week. She wondered dully what James wanted of her. Since, obviously, he did not want *her*, it was probably something quite trivial. She did not hurry. Now that Jai was on the road to recovery nothing seemed very urgent except her need for sleep. She sipped her coffee and decided that she felt like a clock that had run down and was faltering to a stop. She was still smiling faintly at the foolish notion when she joined James in the library.

His first words banished any further notion of smiling and shocked her wide awake. Having once made up his mind he came straight to the point. "My child, I have come to realise that I did you a grave injury in persuading you to marry me against your will. I do not ask you to forgive me for my selfish folly but I will do what I can to make amends. A marriage which has not been consummated may be annulled. I will get Anderson to enquire how this may be achieved with the least noise, for I know that you will not want any breath of scandal to touch you, for your sister's sake rather than for your own. Meanwhile it will be better if we part. If you would prefer to remain here, I will leave. It would probably be better that way. I could go up to Town and consult Anderson without loss of time."

During the past weeks Russet had endured a good deal with commendable self control. She had suffered abduction and captivity; had known the heights and depths of love and despair, the fear of death and loss. Now, in her weariness and weakness she could endure no more. She stared at him dumbly, hopelessly. Great tears began to slide down her cheeks. She put out a hand blindly, fumbling for some support as the sobs shook her body, and found herself caught against his breast, his cheek against her hair as he groaned, "Rosetta! My darling! My little love! Don't cry so, I beg of you. I can't bear it. I deserve to be horse-whipped and hanged, but I promise that I will set you free as soon as it can be done. You need never see me again. Only please stop crying. You will make yourself ill."

Fortunately most of this singularly stupid speech went unheard. The first half dozen words had been enough for Russet. She lifted a very watery face to his, still not quite able to believe that she had heard aright. "*What* did you call me?" she demanded on a gulping sob.

He looked puzzled for a moment, then took her meaning. "I'm sorry," he said simply. "I know I have no right. But even though I set you free, I cannot stop myself from loving you. You need not heed it."

"You love me," she half whispered, wonderingly.

"With all my heart. I think I have loved you since you turned my bones to water walking along that ledge. But the knowledge need not burden you. You shall go free, I promise."

He seemed to have forgotten that he was holding her in his arms, as close a prisoner as she had ever been. Russet made no protest. She felt very comfortable, very much at home. She said slowly, "You are very lavish with your promises, sir. But I made some promises, too. And I mean to keep mine. You cannot get rid of your bad bargain so easily. We are pledged to each other for better or for worse. Before you start making any more promises, don't you think we might try to discover which it is?"

The arms which had been holding her so gently tightened suddenly. Her eyes, still wet with tears, but alight now with laughter, met his incredulous stare.

"You mean it?" he said slowly. "After all I have done? You will stay with me?" And, as she nodded vigorously, "Accept me as your true husband?"

She managed to free one hand from his comprehensive hold and put it up to caress his cheek. "Till death us do part," she said soberly, remembering how close death had come.

His hold slackened as he, too, remembered. "There is still one thing you don't know," he said reluctantly. "If you can forgive me that"—and put her from him, lest her tempting nearness led him to speak less than truth.

Out it all came. How the idea had come to

him when she had tended him so devotedly in his genuine weakness. How, in truth, he had not greatly cared whether he lived or died—which won him a disapproving frown—and how he had deliberately gone without food to hinder his recovery. He had at least the grace to look shamefaced when he came to the carefully staged scene in which he had announced the provisions of his will.

He studied her expression anxiously. She looked startled—shocked—but not wholly disgusted. A little encouraged he went on more confidently, "It worked, too, though I certainly didn't expect you to fly into such a tantrum. And though I am ashamed of myself *now*, I cannot be wholly sorry that I did it, nor promise that I would not behave just as badly again if a similar need arose. I did not know that I could sink to such depths of duplicity. But neither did I know that I could need anyone as badly as I needed you to complete my life. Do you think that you can find it in your heart to forgive me?"

She tried very hard to look suitably severe, a difficult task with happiness running riot in her veins. "It was a *dreadful* thing to do," she told him sternly. And then, swiftly, "And you must never, never, tell anyone else. Poor Phoebe! Imagine her distress if you confessed to such a trick. As for me—I have no choice, have I? For better, for worse, you recall. And to speak truth," she smiled up at him, "I'm very glad you did it. We should not else be married, should we? And think what a shocking waste of time that would mean." And Mrs Cameron looked demurely up at her husband in a most inviting way.

"That, my girl," he told her, "is downright provocation. If it were not for your looking so wan and sickly as you have done this week past, I might take you up on it. And what, may I enquire, is the reason for your sickly looks? Never tell me you were pining away from love of me?"

"I should tell you no such thing, even if it were true," she said indignantly. "You are quite sufficiently conceited as it is." But her eyes told a different tale and she went on slowly, "I suppose I had better confess that you are not the only one with a guilty secret. Though mine is perfectly respectable. And like yours it has a happy ending." And she told him of Jai's illness and of how she and Heaton had nursed her back to convalescence.

As the tale progressed he gathered her back into his arms, punctuating her words with light kisses on hair and brow and cheek, revelling in the sense of possession but his eyes very tender. "Perfectly respectable, indeed," he agreed quietly. "But no more secrets, love, however respectable, and no more playing tricks with your health. You are much too precious."

"Well! Of all the infamous things to say! *You* to talk of playing tricks with one's health!"

Since this reproach was perfectly legitimate Mr Cameron could think of only one way of silencing it. This method he adopted with enthusiasm. No more was heard from his wife for quite some time, and when she did speak it was on a different head.

"You didn't mean those horrid things you said about leaving me behind when you went to Scotland?"

He grinned. "First you must be carefully nursed and restored to your usual good health," he told her solemnly. "Milk possets and early bed times. Especially early bed times," he added thoughtfully, so that she blushed. "Then we shall see about taking you to Scotland. There's no great haste. We shall have time for a honeymoon before Joanna's wedding."

"And shall I like that?" she enquired with innocent interest.

"You must *try* to do so," said her much teased spouse solemnly. "It will be difficult for you, I am aware. You will be obliged to put up with a great deal of my society and to accept at frequent intervals such tokens of my esteem as I bestowed upon you just now. However, in view of the fortitude with which you accepted those same tokens I by no means despair of a happy outcome. You may even find yourself actually deriving some small enjoyment from the exercise. I have heard that this is perfectly possible if one is sufficiently practised in the art."

She was staring at him in amazement. He had always been so serious, so restrained, his humour dry rather than playful. She had not dreamed him capable of such nonsensical speech. But her heart rejoiced at the realisation that the future would be seasoned with laughter and teasing.

He went on, in the same pontifical vein, "Practice, of course, must be commenced during the early days of the honeymoon and repeated as often as may be convenient. And the present time and place," he reverted suddenly to his normal manner, "seem to me to be excessively convenient. So come here, Mrs Cameron and let us endeavour."

And Mrs Cameron, that meekly obedient wife, shaking with laughter, obligingly did as she was bid.